# WITH MY LI[       ]LE

Francis King is a former International President of PEN and drama critic of the *Sunday Telegraph*. His fiction includes *Act of Darkness*, *Dead Letters* and *The Custom House*. Arcadia published *Prodigies* to great acclaim in 2001, while his 28th novel *The Nick of Time* was longlisted for the Booker Prize 2003.

# FRANCIS KING
# WITH MY
# LITTLE EYE

ARCADIA BOOKS

Arcadia Books Ltd
15–16 Nassau Street
London w1w 7ab

www.arcadiabooks.co.uk

First published in the United Kingdom 2007

A catalogue record for this book is available from the British Library.

ISBN 1–905147–27–9

Designed and typeset in Minion by Discript Limited, London wc2n 4bn
Printed in Finland by WS Bookwell

Arcadia Books Ltd acknowledges the financial support of The Arts Council of England.

Arcadia Books supports English PEN, the fellowship of writers who work together to
promote literature and its understanding. English PEN upholds writers' freedoms in
Britain and around the world, challenging political and cultural limits on free
expression. To find out more, visit www.englishpen.org, or contact
English PEN, 6–8 Amwell Street, London ec1r 1uq.

*Arcadia Books distributors are as follows:*

*in the UK and elsewhere in Europe:*
Turnaround Publishers Services
Unit 3, Olympia Trading Estate
Coburg Road
London n22 6tz

*in the USA and Canada:*
Independent Publishers Group
814 N. Franklin Street
Chicago, IL 60610

*in Australia:*
Tower Books
PO Box 213
Brookvale, NSW 2100

*in New Zealand:*
Addenda
Box 78224
Grey Lynn
Auckland

*in South Africa:*
Quartet Sales and Marketing
PO Box 1218
Northcliffe
Johannesburg 2115

Arcadia Books is the *Sunday Times* Small Publisher of the Year

FOR STEPHEN SIMPSON

Champion of books and kindest of friends

*The living are the dead on temporary reprieve*

# (1)

I spy!

I lie on my side, right hand under cheek, and in the twilight I peer through the tunnel choked with trails of dead or dying vegetation. I shut one eye and attempt to focus the other. Then I reverse that process, shutting the other eye. I hear the whimpering on the other side of the curtain on my left but I pay no attention to it or to the accelerating patter of heels on the linoleum and the nurse's impatient 'Well, what is it?' Sometimes instead of that whimpering I hear only a reiterated 'Mum, Mum, *Mum*!' occasionally interrupted by 'Mum, where are you? *Where are you?*'

I spy!

The tunnel has become a telescope. I peer through it. Spotted and smeared, it needs drastic cleaning. I see her, motionless, unwinking in her stare, her eyes blue beads of glass. She is huge, as though transformed like Alice in Wonderland by some magic potion. She rises from her haunches and, eyes still fixed on me, she pads down the telescope – or is it now once again a tunnel? – towards me. I wait for her with a sudden upsurge of relief. She has come to me, my American Rag Doll, risen from the mound of earth at the far end of the narrow, neglected garden. She has come back from the dead. She approaches my bed, halts, squats. She tilts her head up at me and I raise my head. We stare at each other. Then suddenly she bounds. She is there beside me, no longer the size of a tiger but touchingly small, as once I knew her.

I feel no surprise. I put out a hand and stroke. Her coat is soft and warm, not matted and damp as during those last days when she lay stretched out on her side, an emaciated near-corpse, on the bed. Laura did not want her there – *no, no, not on the bed, not on the bed*! Not merely my hand but my whole body begins to vibrate as she purrs. I stroke again. The purr becomes the core of my being, like some engine driving a ship through a calm ocean while its passengers lie sleeping.

Then suddenly it ceases. I half sit up and extend my hand, searching for her. I peer through the tunnel-telescope, straining to see past the trails of dead and dying vegetation to the far-off light at the end of it.

She has gone. I am alone again. Once more I hear that whimpering. Once more I hear that terrified, desolate 'Mum! Mum! *Mum!*' from the man with the red-rimmed, madly darting eyes and the parrot-beak nose, even more ancient than I am.

⌒

I ask myself: Why am I here? Then I ask myself: What happened? I remember a man raising an arm and a television screen obstinately flickering before flashing into life. That is all. When? Where? How?

'Don't worry about it. It'll all come back to you.' That's what Laura says to me. That's what everyone says to me. That's what I even sometimes say to myself.

⌒

'Well, how are we this morning?'

Dr Szymanovski's question is perfunctory. He is squat, with disproportionately large, peasant hands, and a face already creased and grey with weariness. When he first told me his name, I asked him if he was related to the Polish composer. He shook his head, pulling a small face, his jaws moving from side to side, tongue exploring, as though he had unexpectedly found a splinter of bone in a mouthful of stew. 'Everyone asks me that.' This morning a spindly young man with a prominent chin and kind eyes accompanies him.

'Much as I was yesterday. Except that something odd has happened.'

'Odd?' He peers down at my file. This is merely a routine. He isn't really interested.

'I've been having what I can only call hallucinations. Our cat. Our dead cat. I keep seeing her.'

He jerks his overlarge head up from the file and his small, wary eyes scrutinise me. 'Bonnet.'

'Bonny?' I am bewildered.

He turns to the young man. 'Explain. Tell him about Bonnet's Syndrome.'

I know already – as Dr Szymanovski knows, I am sure – that the intern has no idea what Bonnet's Syndrome is.

2

The intern gives an embarrassed little cough and clears his throat. 'Sorry. I haven't the faintest.' The accent is Scottish.

Dr Szymanovski is pleased with that ignorance. He smiles. As his lips part I note for the first time the small tuft of gingery hair under his lower lip. Did he deliberately leave it unshaved this morning or did he merely overlook it? 'I didn't think you would. Way back in the eighteenth century, there was a Swiss physician called Bonnet. His father – a tough old boy, as sane as could be, not in the least imaginative – had a stroke, like you, and then began to have hallucinations. Like you. Bonnet investigated the phenomenon.' He turns away, hesitates and then turns back reluctantly. 'So you see your dead cat? Nothing else?'

'Nothing.'

'Anything frightening about that?'

I shake my head. 'No. In fact – it's somehow comforting.'

'Well, you're lucky. Not long ago I had a patient – a household name but of course I can't reveal it. Well, he started to see knives – sometimes dripping blood – and even people brandishing them. That went on for several weeks. Your cat may go on visiting you for several weeks. Nothing to worry about. It'll pass.'

'And my sight. This tunnel vision. Will that ever return to normal?'

He shrugs. He has enjoyed talking about Bonnet's syndrome, I am sure of that, but now he is embarrassed. In any case he must move on to the bed of the emaciated, whimpering old man next to me and to innumerable other beds. I have already had far more than my ration of his invaluable time. 'Who knows? I don't.' He shrugs his pugilist's shoulders. 'We can only hope for the best.'

I peer through the tunnel at the two receding figures, the squat consultant and the lanky intern. Then, as they grow tinier and tinier, I see beyond them, squatting motionless with unblinking, blue glass eyes, the cat, my beautiful American Rag Doll, far larger than they are.

Indifferent, they walk through her and away, rubbing her out of existence.

⌐

She – my long-suffering, long-suffered Laura – stoops over my bed and holds out a bottle. 'Look what I've found for you.' It is many years since I've seen such a bottle, chunky and square. I don't have to peer at the label with my little eye. With extraordinary clarity I remember it. POUR UN HOMME. Then in smaller lettering, no capitals, *eau de toilette*. Then below that CARON, and below that again *Paris*. She twists off the hexagonal black top and holds the bottle out towards me. 'I remember how much you loved your Caron all through that hideous Japanese summer. Frankly I came to hate it.'

I breathe in the dizzying, now slightly nauseating scent, my eyes shut. Mmm! Then I gasp, open my eyes wide and smile at her. It is years since I used that scent. But during that time in Japan way back in the sixties when everything – even the cushions on the two facing sofas, the pillows on our bed, the towels on the rail – seemed to be damp and stinking of sweat, I was constantly splashing that liquid under my arms, over my palms or on to a handkerchief to press against my forehead and cheeks. Even after a shower or a shave I would use it. When, with increasing rarity, I made love to her, I would rub it all over my body in preparation. The Caron was my drug. It was also my aphrodisiac. Under its brief influence I ceased to be aware of the vast simmering cauldron in which we were trapped and that vinegary stench of sweat and putrescence that seemed always, inside and outside the house, to envelop us. 'You stink like a brothel!' she would say, half in derision, half in disgust. Or, 'Anyone would think you were a nancy boy, the way you douse yourself in that stuff.' Those were the days when even young people like her with defiantly progressive views talked of nancy boys.

She screwed back the top and placed it on my bedside table. 'I hope people won't mistake you for an old queen.' Once it was nancy boy, now old queen.

'It was kind of you to bring it.' I put out a hand and take hers. I feel her wedding ring and turn it one way, then the other. Worn but indestructible. Like our marriage, I think sentimentally, not with entire truth. 'A lovely and unexpected present.'

'So how are things?' She sits down on the chair beside my bedside table and stoops to take a package out of the capacious bag at her feet. 'I made you some smoked salmon sandwiches.

And I've brought you two cakes from Bonne Bouche. Has there been any improvement in the food?'

'None. But I don't really mind. I've got no appetite.'

'Are you sure you don't want to move?'

'Yes, sure.'

'But it's so dreadful here. No privacy. Noise. Ghastly food.'

'All that doesn't worry me.' But in fact it does. What keeps me in this ward is a vestige of socialist principles that, like my young self, were once headstrong and vigorous and now, again like myself lying here, are acquiescent and feeble.

From the bag she draws out her knitting. It's yet another pullover for me. She frowns down at it, holds it up and peers at it, then rests it on her knees. For days and days, all through that hot summer until her cruelly abrupt departure, she would either lie motionless in our air-conditioned bedroom or else sit out on the terrace under the tattered persimmon tree, the baby beside her, and knit relentlessly and indefatigably on and on and on. Then, suddenly, she in effect jumped to her feet, dropped the knitting, snatched the baby from his pram and vanished. 'I just can't stand this any more. He can't stand it either.' Those were what I remember as her last words, but there were many more, no less devastating, after them.

Even in that terrible heat she was beautiful. Even in her seventies she is beautiful now. Her hands at the knitting are those of the thirty-two-year-old woman, rich, impatient and capricious, that she was then. Her face, with its high cheekbones and broad forehead, legacies, along with the wealth, from her Ukrainian grandmother, is so free of wrinkles that one of her female American cousins, on a visit to us from New York, once asked me whether she had had plastic surgery. *No, no, of course not*! Indignantly I repudiated the idea.

I wonder whether I should tell her of the return of Smoky, our American Rag Doll, from the grave. Not now I decide. She is worried enough already. To be told that I am hallucinating would worry her even more.

As, with that slightly limping gait, the result of an accident on a tricycle in her childhood, she eventually walks away from me down the tunnel that leads her past the long, receding row of beds and then through the swing doors, I suddenly see the grey-brown, yes *smoky*, shadow accompanying her, close to her left ankle, all but touching it.

Then both of them pass through the door.

At that moment I smell with an overpowering intensity the Caron that she has dabbed on my forehead and cheeks. In those long-lost days of summer in Kyoto, it always seemed to me that it was the potent essence of life. Now it has changed, mysteriously, into the no less potent essence of what I recognise as death.

# (2)

I have never been wholly able to recapture the extraordinary exhilaration of those first weeks. I try now to recapture it, as I lie sleepless in the dimly lit ward, hour on hour, in silence broken by only an occasional mutter or moan, the hurried appearance, merely dipping a glance at me as he passes, of a diminutive Filipino night nurse, and a disturbance when the Moroccan opposite to me, a cook in a Soho restaurant I overheard him telling another patient, manages to spill his urine bottle and so drench his bed.

The April sun seemed always to shine, the temperature seemed always to be warm, and – rare in Kyoto, I later discovered – the air seemed always to be dry and clear. Our baby Mark seldom cried and the skin of his face, later so often red and crumpled by fever and the heat, was then smooth and strangely luminous, as though an invisible lamp were shining down on it with a soft, even light. I used to put out a hand to him and he would clutch one of my fingers with a grip that amazed me with its strength. It seemed to parallel the constant feeling that I had that now, for once, at long last I had myself achieved a firm grip on life.

With my meagre British Council scholarship I had little money. But Laura, then as now, had a lot of it. When I married her, there were friends who clearly thought that I had done so in part – perhaps even in major part – because of all that money flooding in from family trusts and the shrewd investment of millions, literally, left to her by her grandmother. But when we had first met, she had been living so simply and economically in a one-room flat in an inconveniently remote and dingy mansion at the far end of the Banbury Road, its Edwardian façade all but invisible behind rampant ivy, that I had assumed that, struggling to reconcile a tireless social life with completing a thesis, she must be as hard up as I was. That thesis, on 'Time and Place in the Novels of Ivy Compton-Burnett', had long since begun to bore her, as it would certainly have bored her examiners, and she was soon to abandon it. That I did not give up on my certainly no less boring one on Uchida Iwao, Western-style painter and social-realist writer, was what had brought us to Japan.

A friend, a lecturer at SOAS, clearly unaware of how rich Laura was, had recommended to us a *pension* kept by an elderly Russian woman, an aristocratic émigrée known to everyone merely as Katinka, and her Japanese husband. We argued about whether to go to there or, as Laura could well afford, to opt for the Miyako Hotel. Then, on a whim, Laura decided, as she decided most things between us, that it might be 'fun' to go to the boarding house rather than to a 'stuffy five-star palace'.

At least twenty years younger than she was, Katinka's Japanese husband, a former waiter, shuffled around, hunch-backed and silent, in a pair of Western-style carpet slippers trodden down at the heels, as he performed, in what appeared to be slow motion, the few simple tasks that she, always so commanding and energetic, allotted to him. There were seven rooms and a dozen or so guests, the number depending on how many of them shared. People previously strangers to each other would often opt for reasons of economy to be cooped up in the same little wooden box, where they would at once start to get on each other's nerves. Some of them were students, some youthful transients.

An elderly American couple, the Shotts, had for a consider-able period occupied what was to all intents and purposes a small flat, part Western and part Japanese in style, at the far end of the building. Ignoring Laura's attempts to be friendly, they tended merely to nod to us without speaking when we met at the entrance or passed each other in a corridor. Even indoors he always wore a tartan cap pulled down low over his forehead, and carried a heavy stick, as though not so much to support his sturdy frame as to beat off any potential assailant. What she almost invariably wore were ankle socks on her otherwise bare, scaly legs. Under one arm there would usually be a book – borrowed from the nearby British Council library, we eventually learned.

Why and how they had washed up in Kyoto, it took some weeks to learn. Unlike the rest of us, they prepared their own food and so at mealtimes never entered the long, low communal dining room, with its decommissioned brass samovar on a doily-covered table at one end, and its hatch to the kitchen at the other. But as we walked past that room at other hours, we would often glance through its open door to see them sitting on unyielding upright chairs at one of the three large, circular tables, while talking with a feverish animation to Katinka – or Mrs Katinka, as the Japanese usually called her. Their raised voices and uninhibited laughter reverberated down the corridor in pursuit of us. What had they to say to each other? Why, so detached and silent when running into us, were the Americans now so rowdy and jolly?

In that dining room Katinka's husband would serve us the surprisingly delicious food, much of it of the country of her origin, that she cooked for us in a chaotic kitchen. Even now I remember her wonderfully tender liver in sour cream, her pork chops with beetroot, and above all her Malakoff cake, served in slices so generous that we would often wrap halves of them in our paper napkins to consume later in our room. As her husband sidled between the tables, he would continually blink his eyes, turn his head from side to side as though his neck were stiff, and give strange little nods at no one in particular.

We soon decided that we must move. But we put off doing so while I followed up introductions, investigated the libraries and galleries, and wandered the city, still little damaged by speculative greed and the ever-rising flood of tourism, in a tingling daze of happiness and wonder. Sometimes Laura, leaving Mark to the care either of Katinka or of some female student among our fellow lodgers, would accompany me. But most often I was alone. I preferred it that way. That I should do so puzzled and worried me. In England I often felt bereft even when merely going for a short Sunday afternoon walk in Holland Park or Kensington Gardens without her.

One morning Laura, having got out of our sagging, iron-frame double bed and thrust a foot into a slipper, suddenly stamped out at something. A cockroach was scuttling across the worn linoleum floor. 'Got it!' she shouted at a second stamp. The smashed corpse was now oozing what looked like a yellow-green pus. Cockroaches were always with us, furtive and repellent, as were tiny lizards, seemingly encrusted with emerald dust as they either rested immobile near the top of the rickety wardrobe or flickered up a wall. She pulled a face: 'We really must do something about getting out of this dump.' When we had complained about the cockroaches to the Russian woman, she had tossed her head: 'You must learn that in Japan cockroaches are a way of life.' By then we knew that she did not care for us or think much of us, however effortfully we tried to charm and please. But she adored Mark, holding him in her arms and crooning to him in Russian, her usually implacable face suddenly irradiated with pleasure and love.

A few days later something happened that disturbed us and puzzled us. As we were returning from the communal Japanese-style bath at the back of the house, Laura put a hand into a pocket of her dressing gown. She drew out an object and stared down at it. Then she let out a squeak and let the object drop. A dead cockroach. Had the creature crawled into the pocket and died there? That was the most reasonable explanation. But neither of us could then be reasonable. We asked each other: Might the Russian woman have put it there? Might one of the lodgers have done so? All her life Laura has suffered from sudden bouts of paranoia, sometimes mild, sometimes acute but mercifully as transient as her migraines. On this occasion the paranoia was acute. 'Someone is trying to get at us,' she said more than once over the next few days. Finally she expressed the fear, at once ridiculous to me and yet vaguely disturbing, that the planting of the dead cockroach might have had something do with black magic. 'Black magic?' I expostulated. She nodded. 'Why not? What you've still not grasped is that, though this is in some external ways an extremely modern country, it's also, at its heart – its dark heart – an extremely primitive one.'

As always on such occasions, I did not try to argue with her.

⌒

At that period estate agents seemed not to exist in Japan. We therefore decided to ask if someone at the British Council could help us. On our knocking on his door, the plump, narrow-shouldered, wide-hipped, middle-aged director, Rex Cauldwell – homosexual, we were later to learn, after he had befriended us – opened it, grinned at us, revealing widely spaced teeth and then, when told of our errand, tilted his round head, with its dandelion clock of hair so blonde as almost to be white, to one side and said, 'Alas, alack, you've come at a bad time. I'm afraid you've caught me while I'm working on my files.' I could see no files, only an airmail copy of *The Times* spread out on a desk bare but for a half-full in-tray and an empty out one. 'Mrs Iwai may be able to help you. In fact I'm sure she can.'

Mrs Iwai, with her pageboy haircut, startling pallor and American accent, was only too willing to do so. It was soon obvious that, with her domineering air and brisk efficiency, it was she who really ran the office. Thinking that, because I was on a scholarship, we must be short of money, she at once came up with a number of totally unsuitable premises that, it soon became clear, belonged to people either related or known to her. Some of these flats gave the impression of having been created for dwarfs. Others were in rickety Japanese houses, all paper and friable wood, which seemed in danger of imminent collapse into the narrow, overcrowded streets on which they were situated. Laura would vigorously shake her head or exclaim, 'No, no, no!' even before we had entered such buildings, and then as often as not would turn round and retreat up the street, regardless of our appointment with the owners or whoever was acting for them. It was I who would then have to make our peace.

Eventually, returning home even more tired and disheartened than usual, we told Katinka of our problem. After some thought she mentioned three properties, one several miles out of the city on the road to Nara, one with only one Japanese-style bathroom to be shared between two flats, and one with no bathroom at all, so that it would be necessary to trek out to the public bath – 'Not more than five minutes away, in Japan the custom of the public bath is usual,' she added airily. After we had shaken our heads and demurred at each suggestion, she sighed, 'You are difficult folk.' She pondered for a while, frowning, a hand to the red bandana that she always wore wrapped around her narrow temples. Then in self-reproach she knocked on her forehead with arthritic knuckles. 'Foolish me! There is Madame Kawasaki. Residence in Kitashirakawa. Beautiful, expensive neighbourhood. Bought for her son, now maybe, yes, in South America. Brazil. But too expensive, I think.' She sighed. 'Perfect home.'

'Might we see it?' Laura asked eagerly.

'Sure. But very, very expensive. Not for you, I think.'

'Never mind. Please, could you put us in touch with this lady?'

Katinka looked down at her scuffed, scarlet bootees with their perilously high heels, shrugged and looked sideways and away from us. Then she stared at Laura for several seconds, eyes almost closed, before saying, 'Sure. If so you wish.'

⌒

That evening Laura, pushing the pram, and I with a Leica that she had recently given me for my birthday dangling from my neck, came face to face with the American couple, as we were going out and they were coming in. For once, to our surprise, we were accorded an unmistakably friendly smile from her and a 'Hi, there!' from him. Although 'Hi' is not a greeting that I often use, I repeated it in response, adding, 'It's such a lovely evening that we decided to give an airing to our little one.'

'Well, have a good time! We've just had our daily airing.'

As we approached the wicket gate on its creaking hinge, we heard the man's voice from behind us: 'Hi there! One moment!'

'Yes?'

The couple had turned back from the door and were now once more approaching.

'I meant to say,' he began. 'Katinka has just told us. You're going to view Mrs Kawasaki's house?'

'It's just beautiful,' his wife put in.

'One of the most handsome in the whole city,' he confirmed.

'When we first came here – oh, some years ago now – we stayed there for some months. Large rooms and many of them. A huge, really *huge* terrace.'

'And a real yard. Not the usual poky little Japanese one,' he took up. 'There's this persimmon tree...'

'But sadly we had to leave and come here. We just couldn't afford it. Mrs Kawasaki was charging us far too little and so we couldn't really complain when she said she was going to have to up the rent.'

The old man pulled off his cap to reveal a fringe of grey hair circling a creased area of baldness never before revealed to us. The action suggested a suddenly achieved intimacy. He raised a hand and scratched the scalp vigorously, almost viciously.

'We're retired,' he said. 'I was in the army commissariat here during the occupation and it seemed a good idea to stay. We had fallen in love with the people and everything was so cheap. But things that once seemed cheap no longer do so when you're living on a pension.'

'We were so happy in that house. It was like a palace to us.'

'Even though it was, well, kind of sombre.'

'Sombre?' The word surprised me. In Kyoto nothing at that time seemed sombre to me. Everything was so vivid and so ravishing. The cherry trees in blossom on either side of the unpaved lane that led from the boarding house to the main road seemed to have been covered in a sudden fall of snow. The light glittered off their branches. The sky at that particular hour of the evening was cloudless and clear, with the sun – half of a huge orange disc – about to disappear beneath the far, misty horizon.

'Yeah. Well, I don't how to explain it. We never really felt at home there.'

'No, it wasn't exactly *homey* there. Maybe it was too grand for us really to feel at home there. But we loved it, we just loved it. We'd never lived in that sort of house before. And we never will again, that's for sure.'

He thrust out a hand. 'We've never learned each other's names. I'm Erwin. Erwin Shott. And this is my wife – well, you already must have guessed that – Lucy Shott. And you're...?'

I told him, stumbling over our names as, oddly, I so often do when asked for them.

'Well, it was nice to talk to you,' Laura said. 'We must push on, I suppose.'

Mrs Shott stooped over the pram. 'She's just gorgeous!'

'Not she,' I corrected. 'He. Mark.'

'Oops! At that age it's *so* difficult to tell... Oh, he's *so* cute.'

'We always wanted a baby of our own,' the man took up. 'We tried and tried.'

The woman sighed. 'We decided that that was God's will.' She sighed again. 'Well, He's given us so many compensations. We must just be thankful for all of those.'

Laura, with her usual impatience, put a hand to the pram. 'We must push on I'm afraid,' she repeated.

'Sure, sure!' That was the man. 'Push away!'

'And don't forget to tell us how you get on with Mrs Kawasaki,' the woman called out. 'She's such a fine lady. You're really going to like her.'

'Of the old school. One of those samurai families. Now don't be intimidated! Tell yourselves you're just as good as she is. And don't forget to give her our – well, not love – respects.'

⤶

Their upper stories viewable from the road but their ground floors invisible, the two adjoining residences (that grand word, used by Katinka, seemed appropriate) would not have looked out of place in Brighton's Dyke Road or London's Bishop's Avenue. Mrs Kawasaki owned both. Her father had built the first of them for himself and his family in the immediate aftermath of World War I. She had built the second for her son, her only child. It was in the first of these that she now lived with an elderly maid and occasionally a lodger or two, always female and usually American. There was a high wall around both houses and a low wall between them. The lodgers had their own side entrance and used what had been the servants' staircase in her father's time. She was clearly a woman who both valued her own privacy and respected that of her tenants.

We had thought it odd that, when I had spoken to her on the telephone, she had instructed us in her piping child's voice not to ring the bell of her own house, but to go to the entrance of the other one, where she would be outside waiting for us. Why wait for us outside? As we approached down a long, narrow lane, we saw far off the diminutive figure standing motionless in front of the embossed arch of a wooden door set into the forbidding wall. Sunlight glinted on the bunch of keys that she was holding out in one hand, as though even at that distance she were already proffering it to us. She was wearing a brown, near-black kimono with an *obi* almost as dark, and elaborately embroidered brocade silk *zori* on her tiny feet. Her hair, which must have been dyed, was so black and stiff that it might have come from a horse. During a subsequent conversation that we had had with him, Erwin Shott had described her as 'a Japanese of the old school – and all the better for that.' Now we at once saw what he had meant.

As at our telephone call, I was again surprised both by the childlike timbre of her voice and an American accent so near-perfect that one might have mistaken her for a Nisei. Later we would learn that between the wars she had spent three years in Seattle, as the ward of a childless aunt and uncle long settled there, and had attended an American college. Later still she would even show us and her two American girl student lodgers an album of photographs of a time that, we at once concluded, had been extremely happy for her. In all of them she was a pretty, short, plump teenager in Western clothes, often a dark-blue pleated skirt with a white sailor blouse above it. She was almost always smiling to reveal gleaming, overlarge front teeth.

She stood back, bowing slightly, to let Laura and me through the gate ahead of her. Having not yet become used to this convention of man preceding woman, I hesitated. '*Please*,' she insisted. The child voice had suddenly strengthened and deepened. The forward tilt of her head and her sideways glance at me now projected a compelling authority. 'Thank you,' I muttered, and followed Laura, who had already passed through the gate into the garden.

'Oh, what a lovely garden!' Laura cried out. It was not the sort of cramped garden, full of dwarf bushes, irregularly shaped areas of sand and artfully matched and arranged stones to which we had already become accustomed on our walks around the city and in our visits to people to whom I had had introductions.

'An English garden. That's what I wanted. If you decide to live here, you'll feel at home. Won't you?' Suddenly she glimpsed a shiny fragment of wrapping paper – perhaps from a cigarette packet, perhaps from a bar of chocolate, blown there by a gust of wind – on the perfect lawn ahead of us. With a shake of the head, clearly vexed, she hastened over and stooped to pick it up. She retained it in her small fist until we had entered the house. Then she murmured, 'Excuse me,' and briefly vanished, no doubt to deposit it in a dustbin. Later, we discovered that she had a mania for tidiness and order.

What we had not realised from our first view from the road was that, built on to this Western-style villa there was a low, Japanese-style extension, with paper shutters and a wooden veranda that ran its whole length. In front of the veranda there was an irregularly shaped pond, in which carp glinted momentarily and then vanished. Mrs Kawasaki began to explain this juxtaposition of two such different styles of buildings. After her years in the States, she had become a lover of a Western way of life, indeed of everything Western. But she had also inherited from her father, a collector of Japanese art, a hoard of paintings and objects that she had decided must be displayed in a setting appropriate for them. In building the house for her son, she had therefore instructed its architect that, though it would be in Western style, she must have an annexe to it that was Japanese. When her son and his wife and children had eventually departed, she had then decreed that the tenants that followed them should not enter the Japanese annexe. This was because, even though everything of any real value had long ago been removed for storage in the family *kura* or godown, she thought it prudent to avoid any possibility of damage either to so flimsy a structure or to the artefacts and scroll-paintings that it still contained.

We were later to complain fretfully, as the summer temperature inexorably soared, of the thick carpets and heavy cretonne curtains, the cumbrous sofas and armchairs, and the four-poster bed in the main bedroom with its elaborate swathes of velvet and ruchings of net. But now there was genuine delight in Laura's 'One might be back in England!' She peered at a foxed print of a Constable painting of Salisbury Cathedral on one wall and then turned her attention to an indifferent watercolour opposite to it, of cows out at pasture. Her delight mounted. Off the bedroom there was a dressing room. Perfect for Mark! There was even a washbasin in it. Oh, and there was a *real* bathroom – by that, she meant not a Japanese one, to be used communally, as at the boarding house, but one in which one could lie for as long as one wished, at full length, with high brass taps at one's feet and a rusty shower contraption above one. And in the kitchen – look, look, there was a gas cooker and a *really* large sink! When she opened the door to the downstairs lavatory, she even peered into the bowl to announce triumphantly that the manufacture was English.

'I could make this my study,' I exclaimed in no less delight when Mrs Kawasaki ushered us into a small octagonal tower room at the top of the house. 'Look – one can see Mount Hiei. Well – just.'

Mrs Kawasaki smiled. Unlike the young girl in the

photographs, smiling was something that she did not now do often. 'My son used this room for his research when he lived here. He always said that it was too small. But he loved it.'

'Is he a scientist?'

'Yes, a scientist. Both a scientist and a doctor. He has made some interesting discoveries. His speciality is dermatology.'

Before that she had remained impassive and silent, only speaking when we put a direct question to her and then only perfunctorily. Pride in her son's achievements had animated her.

Our inspection over, she looked first at me and then at Laura, head tilted to one side: 'So – what do you young people think?'

'Wonderful!' Laura said.

I was no less enthusiastic. 'Just what we've been looking for.'

'Now you must go away and discuss it all.' She gave another of those all too rare smiles. 'It's never good to rush into things.'

'But we've made up our minds,' Laura said.

'Don't you first want to...?' Mrs Kawasaki looked towards me.

Laura shook her head decisively. 'I know my husband feels as I do. Don't you, darling?'

'Yes. Yes, very much so.'

I guessed that, despite all her years in America, Mrs Kawasaki was surprised that it should be the wife, not the husband, who was the first to announce a decision as important as this one.

'I don't know if Mrs Katinka has told you the rent?'

'Oh, yes,' I answered. 'Well, an approximate sum. She couldn't be exact, she said.'

Now Mrs Kawasaki named the figure. It was marginally less than Katinka's. 'That's expensive, I know. But houses like this are not common in Kyoto. Western-style, many rooms, furnished, a big garden. A good district. The last tenants – they moved out two weeks ago – were the director of the American Hospital, Mr Anson, and his family. They didn't want to move. But the board decided to build a director's house in the hospital compound.' She smiled. 'It's a smaller house than this, much smaller.'

'Oh, blow the expense!' Laura laughed. 'We so much want it.'

'You've decided already?' Mrs Kawasaki was astonished.

Laura laughed again, this time throwing back her head. 'When can we move in?'

# (3)

It is curious that, washed up in this wasteland by my stroke, I should spend so much of my time thinking of that long-ago seven months in Japan. On the map of my life whole areas of the past are blurred and faded. But that brief period is clear and bright in every detail. It is as though the tunnel vision of my memory is now focused constantly on it. I even have chaotic and frequently disturbing dreams of lurid fragments of it jostling and jangling against each other.

Although it is midday I have just had such a dream. Now it has been abruptly ended by Laura's arrival. She has brought some Scotch eggs and two meringues, prepared by her with all the professionalism that she brings to every task. There has been a problem with the boiler. What is the use of a service contract if no engineer is available for five days? It keeps cutting out and she has to keep restarting it. She is indignant. People highly efficient themselves are always infuriated by inefficiency in others.

No, I can't possibly eat another Scotch egg, I tell her, delicious though they are. Lying like this, immobile except when I totter to the lavatory – mercifully I do not have to rely on bottle and bedpan, like so many of the other patients in this ward – I eat not from hunger but out of boredom. She swings round to face the bed from which the emaciated old man vanished yesterday, in a wheelchair propelled vigorously forward by the cheerful black porter who has repeatedly taken me in the same wheelchair to this or that scan or test. As the chair accelerated down the ward, the old man was still calling out in terror and despair 'Mum, Mum, *Mum!*'

A young Italian – a student at a language school, he has told me – now occupies his bed. He never reads or watches the television suspended above him, but spends most of the time either sleeping or staring up at the ceiling. So far he has had not a single visitor. Laura holds out the box of Scotch eggs to him. 'Would you like one?' He gives a weak, apologetic smile and shakes his head. His chin is dark with stubble and his hair is overlong and unbrushed. 'They're good. I promise you. I made them myself.'

Reluctantly and awkwardly he puts out his left arm. It is shaking violently, whether because of his stroke or because of stress I can only guess. The other arm is limp. He opens his clenched fist, takes one of the Scotch eggs and raises it to his mouth. He takes a small bite, masticates for a long, long time and swallows. He puts his head back on the pillow and again stares for a few seconds up at the ceiling. Then he turns his head and slowly smiles. 'Good,' he says, more in relief than in pleasure. He is still holding the rest of the Scotch egg.

She begins to talk to him, eager, sympathetic and encouraging. Slowly he responds. His eyes brighten and he even laughs from time to time with what strikes me as genuine amusement. Once again I admire her for this ability, totally lacking in myself, to achieve an immediate intimacy with strangers, often of a different nationality or, as now, far younger than she is.

Then he tires. He has spoken to her of his bewilderment when he woke up one morning to find that he was incapable of moving his right arm or his right leg; of the arrival today or tomorrow of his older brother, who will take him back to Italy, to the family home in Modena; of his English girlfriend, who has not been able to visit him because she has a heavy cold and does not want to infect him or the other patients. Now he closes his eyes. 'Poor chap,' Laura says, as though he were not lying there so close to us. 'It's horrible to be ill in a foreign country. One should always be ill in one's own language.'

That, I know, is the reason why, having been consulted as to whether I should stay on in the Japanese hospital or be flown back to England, she opted for the second course, even though she had been warned that it carried a risk.

As she stoops to her large bag to reach for her knitting, I say, 'I wish I knew exactly what happened.'

'But you do know. What more is there to tell you?'

'No, no, I don't know. I know what you have told me and what Miss Morita had told me. But I can't *see* it – in my memory, I mean. It's not part of me, it's outside me. Do you understand what I'm trying to say? When Miss Morita told me

the circumstances, and when you now tell me, I hear what
you're saying but there's a ... a blindness ...'

All at once, like the Italian in the next bed, I feel exhausted. I
find myself wishing that she would go. But as soon as she has
gone, I shall be wishing her back. It's always like that.

# (4)

On that last visit of mine to Japan, a little more than three weeks ago, Miss Morita at once offered herself spontaneously as my unpaid guide. She also did the same thing, forty and more years ago, on my first visit. On that first visit I insisted on paying her. On the second I decided that we had been so close for such a long time that, despite her straightened means, it would have been insulting to have done so.

After almost half a century she is still unmarried; she still covers her mouth with a hand whenever she laughs or, on some occasions, even speaks – a habit that now maddens me since, with increasing deafness, I unconsciously lip-read a lot; she still lives in the same flat, half of a small, tottery Japanese-style house, in which she devoted so much of her time and attention to her ailing mother, now dead for many, many years. There is still a muted yearning in her relationship with me and a quiet ferocity in her dealings with the outside world. Even more now than before, she gets what she wants – on that last visit of mine the opening of a temple usually closed on Tuesdays, the loan of a book that, because of its rarity, must be read in the university library in which it is kept, the immediate repair of my faltering watch. But the will that achieves these successes is always a sword sheathed in a scabbard of apparent modesty and gentleness.

It was she who was with me in that new and strange museum in Osaka when I suffered my stroke. Some premonition must, I am convinced, have made me, pleading exhaustion, at first resist her proposal to go there that morning. But a wave of that steely blade of her will then overcame me – as it had so often done in the past and as the stroke was so soon to do.

We had travelled there – yes, though I have forgotten so much, I do remember that – in the car of the university of which I was an 'honoured guest' (as they repeatedly referred to me as though to convince not merely other people but also themselves that I was someone of importance). Its Japanese driver constantly surprised me with his un-Japanese volubility and vivacity. Clearly he was one of the 'new' Japanese of whom one today hears so much. The squawky middle-aged woman who was, she announced to me, the university's 'International Officer' had efficiently supervised the planning of my programme of lectures, seminars and visits to people expert in my subject; but, 'terribly busy' as she more than once told me, she was happy that, unpaid and efficient, Miss Morita should act as my companion and guide. If the official car were not available, then we would, she kept telling us, be entitled to taxis 'on the house'. 'It's all part of the service,' she added brightly on more than one occasion.

On my arrival at Tokyo airport, Miss Morita, now an elderly woman, and I, now an ancient man, had both felt delight at once again being together. But neither of us showed it. She stood, hands clasped before her and head lowered, behind the 'International Officer' of the university and the director of the department for which I was to give three of my lectures. She did not look at me as I came through the barrier and the other two then stepped forward to greet me. I did not look at her. Eventually, our eyes met. When they did so, I approached her slowly, extended a hand, bowed my head, and, as she took my hand in hers, said, 'How nice to see you again, Miss Morita.' She bobbed in what was almost a curtsey. Her hand was limp and ungiving.

To anyone not Japanese it may seem strange that I should have addressed my assistant, guide and friend of half a century as 'Miss Morita', and that she should have still observed the same formality when addressing me. But that has always been the nature of our relationship – paradoxical to anyone English but of a kind that even today can often exist between close friends and even spouses and lovers in Japan. It has been a relationship that is durable and yet has always kept each of us at a distance from the other. We are closest not on my visits to Japan or hers to England, both increasingly rare, but in our letters. When separated for long periods from each other we have kept up an assiduous correspondence, with my constantly asking her to carry out this or that piece of research for me and her constantly asking me for my critical estimate of this or that

English classic that, slowly turning page after page, she has been reading with her usual scrupulous attention.

What first brought us together, all those years ago, was that, when not tending to the exacting demands of her mother, she was acting as part-time secretary to Mrs Kawasaki. 'Poor girl, she needs the money,' Mrs Kawasaki explained to Laura and me. 'Often I really have little for her to do, but I let her come to me each day in spite of that. I like her. She's a good girl. I feel sorry for her with that mother.' Miss Morita's father, Mrs Kawasaki went on to tell us, had been a junior lecturer in biology at Kyoto University. In his late twenties he had succumbed to the tuberculosis that had already claimed the lives of his mother and a brother – 'hereditary', Mrs Kawasaki explained. The mother came from a once-rich family but now lived largely off her daughter's meagre earnings and a small allowance from a Tokyo cousin with whom she had little contact. She had never fully recovered from a back injury sustained when, attempting to prune some branches of a tree that had begun to overshadow the tiny flat in which she had lived for most of her life, she had toppled off a ladder.

Miss Morita, notepad in hand, accompanied Mrs Kawasaki when we made an inventory of the house. Dressed in a plain brown frock with a white lace collar, brown, low-heeled brogue shoes and a brown straw hat, she was so unremarkable and so self-effacing that I hardly noticed her. 'Six teacups and saucers and six small plates, Imari ware, one saucer cracked,' Mrs Kawasaki dictated, holding up the cracked saucer for me and Laura to confirm. Head bent, peering through her gold-rimmed spectacles, Miss Morita would then scribble frenziedly on the notepad. Later she produced for us a perfectly typed copy of the document.

From time to time, when I met Miss Morita pushing her mother in her cumbrously old-fashioned wheelchair down our long, leafy lane, or hastening to her morning tasks for Mrs Kawasaki, I would give her a bow, murmur a good morning and often add something trite about the beauty either of the weather or of the blossom then all around and above us. She would halt, nod her head and smile. She rarely spoke a word in response. Her mother, a rug over her knees however warm and sunny the weather, would stare at me with an unnerving puzzlement, as though she had never seen me before and had no notion who I was.

It was, ironically, Laura who was instrumental in first establishing a lasting relationship between Miss Morita and myself. During those first weeks of ours in Japan, we had shared an indefatigable eagerness to visit the temples and gardens, all too often empty of all but half-a-dozen or so other people. The farther off that they were situated and the fewer the people who knew of their existence, the more we wanted to see them. We used constantly to telephone Katinka to ask if one or other of her girl lodgers could come over to babysit. On one such occasion, no girl lodger being available, the Shotts turned up – 'No, no, we don't want any payment, we're happy to look after the dear little girl,' Mrs Shott assured us, having forgotten that we had already twice corrected her by telling her that our baby was a boy called Mark.

It was the Shotts who were instrumental in our acquiring a car: an ancient Cadillac with an alternately gasping and clattering air conditioning system, cracked real leather seats and automatic transmission, a rarity in those days, that needed repeated and alarmingly expensive attention. It belonged to an Army friend of theirs, who, not surprisingly, had no intention of taking it back to the States with him. We congratulated ourselves on having got it for six hundred dollars, but its consumption of petrol was insatiable. Laura usually drove. She was astonishingly adroit at edging the huge, clumsy vehicle through what to me appeared to be impassable lanes – 'threading the eye of a needle,' we called it.

Because I spent so much time on our expeditions and so was neglecting the research for which I had been awarded my scholarship, Laura repeatedly urged me to get myself an assistant. 'I'll pay her,' she promised. Since in Japan such posts were far more often filled by men than by women, I wondered why she always used the pronoun 'she'. As so often in my life, I dithered. Then one day, having gone over to Mrs Kawasaki to tell her that a damp patch had appeared on our bedroom ceiling after some heavy rain, Laura burst into my tower study: 'I've had a wonderful idea. Why don't you ask Miss Morita to be your assistant?'

I straightened some papers. 'Oh, I don't really think...' The idea had no appeal for me. 'She's so... so *negative*. Drab.' I laughed. 'And, oh, so plain!'

'Never mind about her looks. Mrs K. says she's highly educated. And she knows a lot about Japanese art. At Doshisha she got a good degree in history and was even offered a university job – which she couldn't take because of that invalid mother. But art is now her great passion in life. According to Mrs K. she's quite an expert on *kashoga* – whatever that is.'

'Genre scenes. Illustrating trades and professions. Well, that's interesting.' I had myself recently become fascinated by the few works that survive of Yoshinobu, a painter who specialised in *kashoga*.

'Well, why not have a word with her?'

For some reason I delayed. Perhaps what I really hankered after was some assistant both beautiful and brilliant. Miss Morita was certainly not the first of those things and I doubted if she would prove to be the second of them.

The next morning, when I was typing out some notes, as always with two fingers, Laura once again burst in, this time with Miss Morita behind her. 'I thought that you really must have a word with Miss Morita about our idea for her. I caught her finishing some typing next door. Do sit down, Miss Morita.' Laura pointed at a chair. Miss Morita edged towards it, stared at its seat as though to make sure that it wouldn't collapse beneath her weight, and then lowered herself slowly on to it. Head slightly tilted to one side, hands clasped in lap and feet crossed at ankles, she then waited for one of us to speak. It was, as so often, Laura who did so.

From Miss Morita's response I at once got the impression that she really did not want either the job or any payment for doing it but was reluctant to say so for fear of hurting my feelings and making me lose face. It was only many weeks later that she confessed to me, over cups of coffee in a cafe, a favourite of hers, in which one tried to be heard against a constant background of classical music, that my making of the offer of work was 'as if someone had – how may I say? – opened the only window of a room after it is shut for many, many years.' She picked up her cup of coffee, sipped daintily and then sipped again. She looked across at me with an unnerving intensity. She licked her lower lip. 'So you understand, sensei, you have saved me,' she eventually brought out.

I was aghast. What had I let myself in for?

In fact, what I had let myself in for was the strongest, most rewarding and most enduring friendship of my life.

# (5)

This morning it was the young Italian whom, at breakneck speed, the boisterous, constantly laughing black porter propelled out of the ward and into the outside world. The Italian's tall, angular, pale brother had arrived, accompanied by a grave and oddly silent boy – the brother's son, another brother? – who must have been ten or eleven, and by the plump, round-faced English girlfriend, constantly sneezing and blowing her nose, who would also be making the journey. I had expected the young Italian to be overjoyed at the prospect of a return to his home. But, strangely, there was a limp, grudging sadness about him. As the others ransacked his locker and then began to pack, the tone of everything that he said to them, whether to give instructions or to answer their questions, was impatient and tetchy.

'*Ciao!*' He raised his good arm to me as he was wheeled past my bed. It was no longer trembling.

'*Ciao!*' I repeated. 'Good luck.'

'Please say goodbye to the signora. And thank her for her kindness.'

The others smiled briefly at me. The brother mumbled, 'Thank you.'

As they moved down the ward, the tunnel through which I watched seemed even narrower and even more choked than usual with snail-smears and trails of dead or dying vegetation. On their disappearance at the far end, I suffered a strange sense of desertion. I had to remind myself that the Italian had been my neighbour for – what? – only four days and during that whole period we had spoken little to each other. I felt that I had known him for a long time. I felt that I knew him well.

Now Dr Szymanovski is walking down the ward towards me. Today he is not in a hurry, as on every other day, and there are two women accompanying him instead of that one Scotsman. I have not seen the Scotsman since that time when Dr Szymanovski humiliated him by asking him to explain Bonnet's

Syndrome to me. Perhaps it is the presence of those two vivid, attractive women, with their bright eyes and ready smiles, that has made the change in him. Now he has clearly cracked a joke, putting a hand on one of the women's arm, since both of them are laughing and he is laughing too.

He asks the usual question. 'Well, how are we today?' He does not wait for my answer. 'Any more of those hallucinations?'

'Not since last I saw you.'

'Super. Let's hope that that's the end of them.' He turns to the two women. 'He was seeing things. Not all that uncommon after a stroke.' He does not ask either of them if she has heard of Bonnet's Syndrome. He would not want to humiliate them, as he humiliated the Scottish intern. As they move off, he is explaining, 'There was this Swiss doctor way back in...' Looking around at the patients, neither of the two women is listening to him.

I stare at the empty bed on which the Italian was so recently stretched out. One of the Filipino cleaners who move about silent and unsmiling has already removed all the bedding. Oddly, even the mattress has gone.

I blink, blink again.

I feel a spasm of terror. I feel a surge of relief.

She is there. Smoky. The pale-blue eyes are looking at me. The extravagant tail fans back and forth, like a gust of smoke from a bonfire. We stare at each other.

I extend my hand. '*Come!*' I say it audibly, not caring if any of my fellow patient-prisoners hear it or not. '*Come!*'

Again I put out my hand. I will her to move towards me.

But suddenly she has vanished.

# (6)

As I end the reading of a book, I always ask myself, 'Did you enjoy it?' Lying awake here, I now put the same question to myself as I edge towards the end of my life. 'Did you enjoy it?'

How can I say no? Having been born white, to upper middle-class parents in a Western democracy and never having been truly hungry and never having endured illness without receiving, as now, efficient treatment for it, have I any reason or right to say no? So, yes, yes, I have enjoyed it. I have known contentment, happiness, and the relief from anxiety, pain and unslaked yearning that is often even more welcome than either of those two. But I wish, oh how often I wish, that I had known more joy.

During those first days in Mrs Kawasaki's residence I knew it every day, as I had rarely known it before and have even more rarely known it since. It was as though, on waking, I had swallowed one of what Laura's constantly miserable and discontented sister calls her 'happiness pills'. In my pyjamas, even before shaving or having my bath, I'd race up the winding stairs to my attic study, hurry over to the round window and gaze out through it, then another little eye, at Mount Hiei as the sun began to turn its previously grey, humped shape an almost luminous orange. Joy would pulse through me. Yes, yes, *yes*! I wanted to cry it out.

Late one evening Laura drove us out in the Cadillac, over what was then an unmade road but is now a busy thoroughfare, to the river at Arashiyama. Three or four weeks ago, almost fifty years after that first visit, I took a taxi out there, also in the evening, with Miss Morita, the two of us sitting decorously, as always, in our separate corners. With mounting horror I saw the buses parked on what had once been an expanse of vivid grass, moistly yielding to one's tread, along the bank of the shallow, sinuous river. There were crowds everywhere; booths selling food, souvenirs and even clothes; and noise blaring from the loudspeakers outside garishly illuminated restaurants.

On that far-off evening with Laura it had all been so different. We had sat for a long time, saying not a word, on a low wall that mysteriously seemed to separate nothing from nothing and gazed out at the dark coil of water streaked with luminescence. At one moment an owl hooted from the trees crowding up and up the jagged mountain on the other side of the gorge. At another moment a geisha, her painted face and the *geta* on which she hobbled along startlingly white against the velvety darkness, and two dumpy, middle-aged men in business suits and ties, no taller than she was, walked past us. She said something in a squeakily metallic voice, and one of the men guffawed. All three halted, conversed for a moment, and then moved on. Again the owl hooted.

Later we found a boat, its lanterns swaying in the wind, to take us to watch the cormorants fishing. Fifty years later, the river was crowded with such boats and the boats were uncomfortably crowded with people. Now our boat was almost alone under the starry sky. One old man rowed, giving a grunt and a deep sigh with each of his strokes. The other beat on the side of the boat with an oar to attract the fish. The three cormorants, still and wary, stood motionless in the prow. They might have been stuffed. One eye of the largest momentarily glittered; then with what sounded like a choked human scream, he dived. Later I had brooded on the possible cruelty of the near-throttling cord that prevented these birds from swallowing their prey. I had also found one of those parallels that seem to one now penetrating and now merely fanciful. Like the cormorants, the Japanese were constantly and obsessively diving – in their case not for fish but for ever-new experiences, ideas and ways of doing things. Like the cormorants, they were astonishingly proficient at snapping up their prey. But something, an invisible cord unforgivingly tight round their psyches, prevented them from swallowing and so truly ingesting what they had caught.

On that night, however, I had no such feelings or thoughts. I took Laura's hand in mine. I put the other round her shoulder and then stroked her cheek with the back of my hand. She turned to me. She was smiling. I smiled back. Joy! But it was a joy totally different from that joy that each morning surged, irresistible as a tsunami, through me as I gazed at Mount Hiei out of the round tower window. This joy was as serene as the river, as yielding as the grass, and as velvety as the darkness all about us.

Later, after Laura had departed with Mark, leaving me alone, I often used to ask myself with a mixture of bewilderment and desolation, what had happened to that joy. I willed myself to attain it. My spirit stretched out in an impossible craving. Then it slumped back, exhausted and defeated.

⌒

'You'll want a maid, won't you?' Laura and I looked at each other, not sure. 'The Hansons had one. English. Yes, English! A good woman. Christian. Before them, she worked for the director of the French Institute. But, well, for various reasons, she didn't get on there. Her name is Mrs Fukuda. Mrs Joy Fukuda.'

Mrs Kawasaki went on for some time about a woman whom she clearly regarded as a paragon. Soon after the end of the war, this Joy, so grimly different from the joy that I constantly felt at that time, had arrived in Japan on board a P & O steamer on which she had been working as a stewardess. At Hong Kong a young Japanese, returning from a year of study there, had joined the ship and had fallen in love with her. His family, with a long history of public service, was horrified. She had none of the necessary education and breeding. Worse still, she was a *gaijin.* Despite all this opposition the young couple married and in rapid succession produced two sons. By that time he had wearied of her and had come to the humiliating conclusion that his family had been right about her. A divorce followed, with his gaining custody of the boys. To ensure that she saw them for a stipulated one day each week, she had stayed on in Japan, working first as a receptionist at American Express and then as a housekeeper.

She would, we were assured, arrive early each morning in time to get our breakfast and would, if her other commitments allowed, agree to stay late – for an extra payment, of course – if we wanted her for a dinner party. She was an excellent cook – American style, since she had worked largely for Americans. She was also, Mrs Kawasaki repeated, still a practising Christian. She seemed to think that this was the strongest recommendation of all, perhaps because she herself was one.

We were to move into the house from the boarding house the following day. We therefore thought it wise to procure the services of this marvel before some other foreigners did so. So eager were we that we asked only as an afterthought, as we were about to take our leave, what sort of pay she would expect.

When Mrs Kawasaki named the figure, I gasped, 'That's an awful lot of money.'

It was not in fact an awful lot of money by English or American standards; but by then I had got used to everything in Japan being cheap.

Mrs Kawasaki laughed. 'You always have to pay for the best.'

'Oh, don't let's quibble about the money!' Laura put in impatiently. That she never did so was something that both impressed me and made me uneasy. If she constantly refused to quibble about money, might she not eventually end up without any?

⤖

Joy was formidable in both appearance and manner. After our first meeting with her, we told each other that, after her bitter experiences with her husband and his family, that was only natural. In her early forties according to our guess, she was far taller than Laura and almost as tall as myself, with large hands and feet and a wide, low forehead. Her eyes were heavily lidded, the eyes themselves dull. Her nose was large and flared; her over-white, over-regular teeth in a mouth that turned down at the corners were clearly false. Her clothes looked as if they might be castoffs given to her by Anson's wife – a cotton dress, held in at the waist by a leather belt with a huge brass snake-buckle, a woollen cardigan, thick cotton stockings, flat-heeled brogue shoes. Her accent was curious. Laura said that it suggested some inept English actress attempting to play a Yankee. I detected something Irish about it.

We at once realised that this was one of those occasions when the possible employee interviews the possible employer, not vice versa. As, with Mrs Kawasaki in attendance, we progressed round the house, Joy had no hesitation in coming out with unfavourable comments on its condition and its contents. That bathroom window, she pointed out, needed fixing, one hinge had come adrift. She had spoken about it to the Ansons but they had taken no action – that was the sort of people they were, never doing today what they could put off to the next. She often wondered how he ever got started on his operations up at the hospital. Peering down at the dusty sitting-room car-pet, she announced that she would need a new Hoover. In the hall outside the kitchen, she jerked open a fuse box. We really ought to have some of those modern fuses installed: the old ones had to be constantly changed by hand instead of being reactivated by a switch. And, oh yes, she must tell us about the iron. It was essential that she had one of those new steam irons. It saved so much trouble.

I did not take to Joy. I was never to do so. But Laura was enthusiastic. She had a feeling that she was just the person that we wanted, she told me more than once. She might be difficult from time to time but she would always know exactly what to do and would then do it to perfection.

In the weeks ahead Joy responded appropriately both to Laura's liking and to my lack of it.

# (7)

*To know also even as I am known?*
*No!*
*To see also even as I am seen?*
*Yes, that's it. If only, if only!*

'Oh, Dr Szymanovski!' I call out after him as he moves on from my bed. 'Sorry. May I ask you something?'

'Yes.' It's almost a grunt.

'I want to you ask you a question. I want you to be absolutely frank. Do you think there's any chance of an improvement in my vision?'

'Well, if you really want me to be absolutely frank, then my answer has to be – no chance at all. It's what we call irreversible.' He turns away and then turns back. 'Short of a miracle.' He hurries off.

# (8)

Another source of joy during those weeks in a house far larger than any house or flat in which Laura and I had ever lived together, was our insatiable appetite for sex and the increasing adventurousness with which we satisfied it.

Laura had just come in from taking Mark for an outing in his pram and I was busy in my tower study. She had switched on the wireless to listen to the news on the overseas service. The news from 'back home', as she called it, now mysteriously obsessed her. Perhaps it was the premonitory symptom of that morbid sense of isolation in a country in which for most of the time, most of the people did most things differently.

Suddenly, seized by an impulse as uncontrollable as a sneeze, I clattered down the stairs. She was stooping over Mark, who lay out on an antique lacquer table, where Mrs Kawasaki and Joy would certainly not have wanted him, while Laura changed his nappy. From behind I put my arms around her waist, pressing against her. My cock stiffened. With a laugh, she jabbed an elbow into me. Then she twisted round and wriggled out of my embrace. In the background I was suddenly aware of the drone of the newsreader's voice.

'No.'

'Oh, come on. You can't leave me in this state.'

She put a finger to her lips.

'What's wrong?'

She whispered, '*She's* still here? She's baking one of her coffee and walnut cakes.'

'Well, so what?'

'She'd only hear us. Or burst in without a warning. If she weren't so proper and pious, I'd be beginning to suspect her of being a voyeur... We'll just have to wait.'

'Oh, hell!'

Now it was she who put her arms around me. 'Darling, I want it just as much you do. But be patient. Please. *Please!*'

It was at times like these that I not merely disliked Joy but,

36

unreasonably and unjustly, actually hated her. Her attitude to us was at once protective and disapproving. The protection was exclusively for Laura, the disapproval exclusively for me.

We had never imagined that, when we were eating alone, she would formally serve us, carrying round the dishes of always, I have to confess, enticing food. When Laura remonstrated that she could just put things down on the hideous stained oak sideboard, from which we would help ourselves, there was a toss of the head and a look of shocked incredulity. 'Oh, no, madam. That's not the way I've ever done it. And' – she gave her odd laugh, as if she were attempting to conquer an incipient attack of hiccups – 'I'm too old a dog to change my ways.'

'Too old a bitch,' I muttered as she left the room.

Laura put a restraining hand on my arm. '*Please!* She'll hear you.'

'Well, let her!'

'We don't want to lose her.'

'Don't we? I certainly do.'

'We'd never find anyone else so dedicated – and so good a cook.'

It would enrage me to hear the two women chattering endlessly in the kitchen or the hall, or on the upstairs landing. I could rarely distinguish much of what they were saying, but one phrase constantly recurred. It was Joy's 'Oh, madam!' The tone in which it was uttered could be one of affectionate reproach, shocked disbelief or uncontrollable merriment. It struck me as disturbing that, whereas Laura was always madam to her, I was never sir. It was as though she knew, without either of us having intimated it to her, that it was Laura who was paying both the rent of the house and her far from negligible wages for slaving away to keep it in what she would call 'apple-pie order'.

On a number of occasions when, over a meal or coffee or tea, Laura and I had a trivial argument about something – the distance of Okayama from Kyoto, the number of the bus from the house to the British Council, the name of Dr Hanson's young Japanese assistant – Joy, if in earshot, would at once intervene to put us right. Should I emerge victor, it was something like: 'I'm sorry, madam, I can see why you think that. But I'm afraid that he' – I was usually no more than he – 'is right this time.' If Laura were the victor, it was: 'You're right, madam, absolutely right, I can't think how anyone possibly could think different.'

More than once I wanted to shout, 'Would you mind keeping your mouth shut? This is nothing to do with you.' But I never did. Instead, I complained to Laura. On one occasion when I did so, she retorted, even more defensively than usual, 'It's perfectly natural that she wants to put two ignoramuses right when they're making fools of themselves. Can't you see that? Think how long she's been immersed in Japanese life. She's so well informed. She's got so much natural intelligence. With the right education she could have been a teacher.'

'From the way she goes on she must imagine she is one.'

One Saturday, leaving Mark in Joy's care, Laura and I decided to take the long trudge up Mount Hiei to a temple, concealed in one of its jagged folds, of which Miss Morita had told us.

'Would you like me to come with you?' Miss Morita had asked. 'I can show you the path. A friend is visiting my mother that day.'

Before I could answer, Laura said firmly, 'It's sweet of you to offer, Miss Morita. But I know you have an awful lot to do for Mrs Kawasaki. We couldn't possibly take up so much of your time.'

'But I'd be happy...'

'No, no! We wouldn't dream of it.' The words had the finality of a lid being slammed down on to a box and a key then being briskly turned.

Later I expostulated with Laura: 'She'd have *liked* to come, poor dear.'

'No doubt. But I didn't want to have her trailing around with us. That whiny voice of hers really gets on my nerves.'

It was then that I knew what I had only previously suspected. Laura liked Miss Morita as little as I liked Joy.

In the kitchen Joy prepared a picnic for us. From time to time she would appear in the doorway of the dark, high-ceilinged sitting room, overcrowded with elephantine sofas and chairs, in which Laura was yet again listening to the Foreign Service and I was scribbling on some long-overdue postcards. 'Would madam like some sardine sandwiches in addition to the ham and the cheese ones?' 'I thought you might take some of the pecan pie left over from last night. How would madam feel about that?' 'Is it just the Coca-Cola that madam wants or shall I put in some sake as well?' She never asked about my wants or wishes.

'Why on earth can't she get a move on?'

Laura made the now familiar gesture of finger to lips. Then she whispered, 'You know what a perfectionist she is.'

'Only too well.'

After twenty minutes or so, I had had enough. I jumped to my feet and strode into the kitchen. 'How are things going, Joy? Are we anywhere near the end?'

Maddeningly, she went on with her laboriously slow wrapping of sandwiches in greaseproof paper. She did not reply. She did not even look up.

'At this rate we'll miss the best of the day.'

'I'm sure madam wants everything just right. We have that in common.' At that moment Laura appeared behind me. 'Sorry, madam, for the wait. But as I was saying to him a moment ago, I want everything to be just OK for you.'

'It always is OK when you do something for us.'

'Thank you, madam.'

At long last she began to pack the rucksack that I had placed for her on the kitchen table. Pulling open its neck, she sniffed and sniffed again. 'I hope it's all right to put food in here.'

'Why? What's wrong?'

At my questions she shrugged her shoulders and made a little grimace. 'Things don't smell quite as they should.'

'What do you mean?'

'Have you had clothes in here?'

'Clothes? No. Well, not for a long time.'

'That might explain it.'

Eventually she hoisted the rucksack, using both of her hands. 'Here we go! I'll help you on with it.' She hefted it on to my shoulders and then gave it a slap so violent that I nearly tottered over. 'I think everything's there.'

'Oh, thank you so much, Joy. What would we do without you to help us?'

'Well, have a good day, madam. Oh, I've put the sun lotion

there with the other things. I don't want madam to get burned. At this time of year the sun is always stronger than one thinks.'

As we trudged, Laura ahead of me, up the narrow, zigzag path, the greenness of the vegetation, the blueness of the sky glimpsed from time to time through the dense, soaring trees and the deafening screeches of birds for most of the time invisible, assuaged my rage at Joy. When the path suddenly broadened, Laura halted, hands on hips, and waited for me to catch up. Chagrined, I realised that, despite her limp, she was, unlike me, not in the least out of breath.

'I'm so glad she didn't come with us.'

'Who? Joy?'

'Oh, don't be silly, darling. I can't imagine Joy carrying all that weight of hers up a mountainside, tough though she is. No, I meant Miss Morita.'

I said nothing. Then I put out a hand and took one of hers in mine. The skin of her hands, so smooth and soft, always delighted me. I gazed at the sunlight glinting on her thick, yellow hair. It was another of Joy's accomplishments that she could 'do' that hair so well, obviating the expense of the little hairdresser who, toting a scuffed Gladstone bag containing her equipment, visited Mrs Kawasaki every Monday.

'Oh, God, you look so beautiful.'

She gave a small smile, walked on a few paces and then halted and turned. Suddenly her hand was down at my cock. She raised the other hand, placed it round my shoulders and pulled me towards her. Our mouths met; then my tongue entered her mouth.

After a few seconds, she was pulling away. 'Perhaps we'd better wait until we've had our picnic.'

High up – not far now, we reckoned, to the temple – we decided that we had found the perfect spot. It was a flat, open space, a plateau in miniature, on which two moss-covered rocks stood close together, by themselves, in a sea of grass of such a vivid green that it was almost luminous.

Laura placed herself on one of the rocks, wriggled uncomfortably and then said, 'This one is all sharp edges. And the other looks no better. I think the ground will be more comfortable. Did Joy put in that rug, as she said she would?'

I rummaged in the rucksack and then dragged out the tartan

rug. 'Yes, here it is.' I spread it on the ground. I bowed and extended a hand in a parody of the sort of Japanese professor that we were by then constantly meeting. '*Dozo!*'

'What about you?'

'Oh, I'll just risk a sore bum.'

I now got out the thermos with the warm sake in it and the two cups, each carefully wrapped in a screw of tissue paper.

'She thinks of everything. I bet the sake is at just the right temperature.'

'Oh, yes, of course!'

She frowned at my ironic, almost jeering tone and bit into a sausage roll. Joy would often describe her sausage rolls as 'one of my specialities', boasting to us on one occasion: 'Dr Anson was crazy about my sausage rolls. He could never get enough of them. I'd put them out on a plate before one of their parties and he'd gobble half of them before a single guest had arrived.' Laura chewed, the sun glinting on her hair through the trees as she gazed upwards. 'Her pastry is just marvellous.'

'Yes, our Mary Poppins has done us proud.' Grudgingly I had to admit it.

Though I had not drunk a lot of it, the warm sake under the warm sun eventually made me feel unfocused and sleepy. I too now stared up into the trees.

'Paradise,' I said.

She nodded. 'Paradise.'

Suddenly we heard an incoherent chattering all around us. A herd of grey monkeys had begun to gather, swooping from the trees above us and loping towards us over the grass.

'Oh, God! Do you think they're safe?'

I laughed. 'Oh, I'm sure they are. Miss Morita warned me about them but said they were perfectly harmless. If one has a dog with one, it's different. Apparently monkeys loathe dogs.'

One monkey, with hanging dugs and a look of patrician disdain – the grandmother of the pack, I decided – had edged so near over the grass that I could have put out a hand to pat her, had I had the courage to venture such an intimacy.

'What do you think monkeys eat? Shall I try a sausage roll?'

'Why not?'

Laura broke a sausage roll into two and then held one half out to the grandmother monkey. Having stared at it for a while with cynical, unblinking eyes, she shot out a paw. In alarm Laura dropped the morsel. The monkey picked it up, stared down at it and then raised it to her nostrils and sniffed. Dropping it to the ground, she turned her back to us in disgust and scampered off. Suddenly all the other monkeys, as though at her signal, also scampered off, leaping with astonishing agility from one branch to another of the trees above us. In a minute or two all of them had vanished.

Both of us burst into laughter.

'So much for Joy's sausage rolls. An instant monkey repellent.' I shifted my bottom uneasily. 'You were right about this rock.' I got up and squatted on the grass beside her. Then I lay full length, my eyes closed and my face once again upturned to the sunlight glittering through the foliage.

'Coffee? She's even thought of that.'

'Not now. Later. I know what I want now.' I rolled over on to the rug, so that our bodies touched. I put out a hand and slid it under her cashmere skirt. The skin was even softer and the hair silkier than the cashmere.

'Please! Anyone might come.' She made a half-hearted, unsuccessful effort to push my hand away. 'Hey! Stop!'

'Have we seen anyone so far?'

'Well, no. But one can never be sure –'

'To hell with anyone!'

She laughed, 'Yes, to hell with anyone!'

Perhaps because, for all our protestations of not caring a damn whether anyone saw us or not, we were nonetheless apprehensive, it was all over in a few minutes. Gasping, I rolled off her. She was buttoning up her blouse. Then she cried out, 'Oh, you've torn off a button. Do look for it! I'll never find another that matches.'

I was about to do what she asked. Then I saw the grey, hunched shape of a monkey – again that old grandmother, I decided – high, high above us. A branch stirred and another, smaller monkey came into view, head cocked as it peered at us with melancholy, appraising eyes. The trees, I realised with amazement, were thronged with monkeys. I pointed. 'Look!'

Laura laughed. 'Well, without our realising, it wasn't *anyone* who saw us. It was the whole monkey world and his wife.'

'Perhaps they've learned something.' I pointed again. I had

suddenly noticed that just above us one of the monkeys was masturbating with an intense, absorbed expression on his face. 'Perhaps that old boy has learned that there are more interesting and enjoyable things to do than wanking.'

It was a long walk, in virtual silence, up to the temple. We had already realised that it must have been abandoned when, from a distance, we saw that every window was shuttered. Slowly we approached the barbed wire that trailed, a rusty metal creeper, up and down, hither and thither. A huge cat, with a bedraggled black and white coat and one ear missing, was lying on the sagging, soggy thatched roof. As we gazed at it, it leapt up, back arched, gave a hoarse growl and bared its fangs. Then it shot off, out of sight.

Far off we thought that we heard the sound of water dripping. Perhaps a spring was near at hand? We tried to locate it but eventually gave up. There was a musty smell everywhere, such as one finds in a room kept locked for many years. It was curious that, out there in the open, with a breeze blowing, it should be so insistent. Suddenly and simultaneously we both turned away and began to hurry back down the mountain.

After we had descended for a hundred yards or so, the previously oppressive atmosphere thinned and lifted. Laura began first to hum and then to sing the Japanese song, *Sakura*, that Joy would often sing to Mark. When Laura sang it in her small, absolutely accurate voice, it always sounded sweetly seductive. Was it because I disliked Joy that, in startling contrast, her rendition of it so often seemed to me harsh, even menacing?

Laura broke off from her singing. 'What a lovely walk!'

'Lovely.'

〜

'I've put out the drinks,' Joy told us, after we had found her with Mark in the nursery. 'He's been as good as gold, an absolute angel. Haven't you darling?' She got to her feet from the wicker rocking chair on which she had been perched by the cot. 'I didn't put out the ice. I wasn't sure when you'd be back.'

'Oh, I can get that.'

The postman had delivered a wodge of letters, fastened with a wide, red rubber band. I read them in turn and then threw them across to Laura. She read them far more slowly than I had done, perhaps because she was far more interested in their contents. Each of us sipped at a Japanese vodka and tonic.

'She's forgotten the olives,' I suddenly realised.

'Odd of her to forget anything.'

'I'll get them.'

My calves ached from the walk as I padded down the corridor to the kitchen, in the slippers into which I had at once changed on our return.

Joy looked up as I entered. Spread out on the large, rectangular kitchen table, its wood scarred here and there as though it had been attacked with a knife, lay the tartan rug from our picnic. Her gaze went down from me to it. She raised an edge of it and stared intently, lips pursed. There was a stain encrusted there. She might have thought one of us had accidentally dropped a dollop of mayonnaise and had then tried ineffectually to wipe it off. She might have thought that one of us had splashed on to it some of the milk that she had included for our coffee. But I knew, with absolute certainty, that she had thought neither of those things. As soon as she had seen the stain, she had realised its origin.

She looked at me with a mixture of disdain and disgust. Then she let the rug slip from her strong, competent hands as though it were something contaminated and contaminating.

# (9)

The comatose man, usually seen through my little eye as no more than a gleaming, yellow forehead and a straggly beard, vanished two nights ago. Was his corpse trundled off in the early hours without any of us realising it? Insomniac that I am, how could I not have noticed?

'Excuse me – what's happened to the old boy opposite?'

Usually the small Filipino male nurse, with the shaven head and the delicate hands, is willing to respond to my questions, albeit sometimes with a pursing of his fleshy lips. But on this occasion he pretends not to hear me. Perhaps he is scurrying off on some vital errand. Perhaps 'dead' is not a word that he can volunteer.

Later, in the evening, the jolly West Indian porter wheels in a middle-aged man with the red, swollen face of a boozer and a salt-and-pepper moustache that dangles like some exotic creeper over the balcony of a mouth too full of prominent teeth. The man trips as he struggles out of the wheelchair, the porter and a woman whom I assume to be his wife supporting him one on either side, and all but topples over. 'Oh, fuck! Bloody hell!'

'Shh, dear!' Unlike the man's, the woman's voice is what a snobbish friend of mine calls 'pish' – by which she means 'not quite posh'. The man's is irredeemably pish.

Now the woman is again here, soon after we have had our breakfast trays removed, with a large bunch of arum lilies.

The man peers at the flowers. 'Ask the nurse for a vase for those. They'll give me an asthma attack as like as not.'

Perhaps, since his voice is so strident in this place of mutterings and whisperings, a nurse has overheard him. At all events one has appeared. 'I'm sorry. I'm afraid we can't have those in here.' To disclaim any personal responsibility she adds, 'There's a rule about flowers.'

'Bloody hell! There seems to be a rule about everything in this bloody place.'

In what appears to be a sudden attack of fatigue, the woman sinks down on the end of the bed, the flowers resting on her knees. I now notice that, though otherwise drably dressed, she is wearing elegant, extremely high-heeled shoes, with straps over the insteps.

'Put those bloody flowers somewhere, why don't you?'

She places them on the floor. Briefly she closes her eyes.

'Perhaps Cathy can do with them,' he continues. 'They'll cheer her up in that hole of a flat of hers.'

'Why she ever moved there beats me.'

'Well, it was bleeding Clive that wanted that, wasn't it?'

Can it be Cathy who later comes to visit him? And is she his daughter? A back-view of her blazing bush of red hair, clearly dyed, makes her already large head look like a chrysanthemum on the stalk of her long, thin neck. She sits on the end of his bed, one bony leg crossed high over the other. 'I could do with a fag! I could really do with a fag!'

'Don't keep saying that! You're already setting me off!'

Once she has gone, carrying the flowers with her, he badgers the nurses. 'Hey! Darlin'! Hey! One more moment!' he calls out to one as she passes. I feel a cruel satisfaction as she ignores him. 'Fuckin' hell!'

His dinner is brought to him by one of the two Polish helpers, sisters by the look of them, who first wheel in the trolleys and then dash around with loaded trays.

'What's this meant to be then?'

The Polish girl is not sure if she has understood or not. She frowns. 'Cod, I think maybe,' she eventually replies in her heavily accented English.

'Codswallop!' She has no idea what he means. She doesn't want to know. She scurries off.

Suddenly he is aware that, instead of getting to work on the tray already set down over in front of me, I am staring at him.

In a challenging voice he calls out, 'Everything all right with you, Granddad? What do you think of this grub?'

'I've seen better.'

'You can say that again!'

# (10)

'Have you visited Byodoin Temple?' Miss Morita asked, pulling off a kid glove and setting it down carefully on the table at which I had been working in the garden, beside the other that she had already removed.

I shook my head.

'Very beautiful.' She twitched at the gloves until, untouching, they lay in perfect parallel. By then I had already noticed her obsession with symmetry.

'If it's fine, we thought that we might go tomorrow. It's not far, is it?'

'No, not far. It was in this temple Gen-Sammi Orimasa committed suicide in' – she put up a hand to cup her mouth and gave an embarrassed giggle – 'oh, I forget! I am stupid! Maybe eleven eighty, eleven ninety. But what you will wish to see is the Ho-O-Do Phoenix Hall. Beautiful!' She broke off there. I had dreaded a long disquisition, of the kind that she often produced on our sightseeing trips together. 'I have not been to Byodoin for a long time – since I was schoolgirl. And that time I was sick to stomach, so I did not really enjoy.'

'Why not come with us?'

Her face lightened, then darkened, as she pondered. 'You are going alone?

'No, no. My wife particularly wants to see it. Dr Anson's wife told her about it – a must, she said.'

'Yes, it is a – a *must*.' She hesitated over the word, clearly strange to her in that usage.

'And your company is equally a must. We'd like that.' In using the plural I was of course lying. Laura would certainly not like it.

She pondered and then shook her head. 'No.' Then, more loudly, 'No. Maybe not. I think that your wife will like to be alone with you. You can take your little baby. He will be happy there. Afterwards maybe you can drive on to Nara.'

'Oh, we want to spend a whole day at Byodoin. Another time. We have to be careful of cultural indigestion.'

She frowned. 'Indigestion?'

I couldn't be bothered to explain. 'Well, think about it. We'd love you to come.'

She sighed, raising a hand and pressing the back of it to her cheek. She tilted her head to one side, her spectacles flashing briefly in the sunlight slanting across the garden. 'I think better not.'

Later Laura was to ask me, 'What on earth do you and Miss Morita find to talk about? I was watching you from the bedroom window – the two of you in the garden. Why does someone still so young wear those old-fashioned straw hats? Before the war hats like that were worn to vicarage garden parties. Can't you get her to appear in something more up to date?'

'I'd not want to change her. I like her' – I searched for a word – '*quaintness*. Somehow it appeals to me.'

'Oh, you do have the *quaintest* tastes!'

It was odd that Laura, usually so tolerant of my friendships with women in the past, should now so clearly be jealous of someone, well, as *quaint* as Miss Morita. But perhaps, with the clairvoyance that she sometimes so alarmingly displayed, she had already foreseen the years and years of close friendship that lay ahead.

# (11)

He calls out, 'Hey! Darlin', Darlin'! Wait a sec!'

The middle-aged, barrel-shaped nurse hurries past, as though she has not heard him. But of course she has. No one, from one end of the ward to the other, could fail to hear that voice.

'*Hey!*' It is almost a bellow of rage. He looks across at me. 'What a bitch!'

Returning some time later, she is either less busy or is guilty about not having previously answered his summons. She stops by his bed: 'Everything all right?'

'Well, I did want something. But now, bugger me, I've forgotten what it was. You didn't want even to pass the time of day with me, did you, darlin'?' His tone has become flirtatious. 'Just shot past. Perhaps all I wanted to tell you was I like the new hairdo. It *is* new, isn't it? Yes, those tints are spot on.' He raises a thumb in approval. 'Is grub on the way? I'm famished.'

'Soon. Any moment now.' He has managed to thaw her out. 'Sorry I was in such a hurry last time.'

'No problem.'

When she has gone, he looks around him, clearly at a loss as to what to do next, and his eyes, small and glinting, alight on me. He raises his hand in ironical salute, as though he were other ranks to my august major general, and shouts across, 'Everything hunky-dory, sir?'

'As hunky-dory as it can be.'

'So what are you in here for?'

'Stroke.'

'You don't look too bad to me. For your advanced years.' He laughs to indicate that this is no more than a pleasantry.

'Well, I'm glad to hear that. And you?'

'Me?'

'What are you in here for?'

He is disconcerted. He hesitates. 'Well – it's really one of those women's things. You know. Something that men don't usually get.' He stares down at his linked hands resting on the tumulus of his stomach. 'But there it is. Rum thing. Bit embarrassing.'

The Polish sisters have arrived with the trolleys of food. He is relieved of the need to say anything further to me.

'Hello, hello! Here are those two gorgeous girls back again! Well, darlin', what have you got for me, eh? How about a kiss for starters? Eh?'

Their faces impassive, the sisters hurry about their tasks. They never respond in any way to him.

'Stuck-up little bitches!' he comments to me later.

# (12)

The rainy season started. I loved it. Laura hated it.

'Oh, look! Just look at this.'

Obediently I stooped to peer into the tall, narrow refrigerator.

'Joy cleaned it only two or three days ago.' She pointed at the grey-green mould, thick on the egg-rack and rimming the top of the salad tray. 'What does one do about that?'

'Get her to wipe it off. Or I'll wipe it off myself.'

She slammed the door shut. 'Bloody damp! Bloody rain!'

Later I stood out on the wooden platform of the veranda and, shielded by its sloping roof, stared out at the downpour. There was something calming and assuaging about that gentle, regular, persistent shush-shush-shush sound and the grey-green, tirelessly falling water against the intense green of the grass, the bushes and the trees, all suddenly luxuriant. I crossed to the edge of the veranda and put out a hand. Soon, in a few seconds, it was overflowing with water, cool and silky soft. I raised the hand and splashed my face, letting the water run down my cheeks to my chin and then to my shirt. I wriggled with pleasure as I felt it seep through to the flesh beneath.

'What are you doing?'

Laura was behind me, her voice again sharp.

'Watching the rain.'

'Don't you mean getting drenched in it?' She stared out morosely. 'Bloody rain! There's another leak in Mark's room, only inches from above his cot. Shall I tell Mrs Kawasaki or would it be better to get someone competent ourselves?'

I shrugged.

'Would you like to go across to her?'

'OK.'

I was about to jump down from the terrace into the garden below when she cried out, 'What are you doing? Are you crazy? You're in your slippers! Put on some shoes and get an umbrella.'

The old woman who looked after Mrs Kawasaki spoke no English. In the hall she began to say something to me in Japanese, then broke off and shrugged her shoulders, with an apologetic grimace.

'Kawasaki Okusan,' I repeated.

Again she shrugged, then shook her head.

A voice called my name from down the passage. 'Here, here!' it added. I walked towards it. I had never been so deep into the house. Mrs Kawasaki always entertained us either in her sitting room or out on the veranda.

This was her bedroom, oddly stark in comparison with a sitting room crowded with unnecessary knick-knacks and pieces of furniture. She was lying on a day bed, propped on a number of pillows. On her lap was a copy of an Agatha Christie novel that she had asked me to borrow for her from the British Council library. Most of her reading was of crime novels in English. 'I'm not an intellectual like my son,' she once confessed to me. 'Good books bore me.'

I hesitated just outside the door.

'Come in! Come in!'

Reluctantly I stepped forward.

'I'm sorry to receive you here. I – I'm not well. Nothing serious,' she added quickly, no doubt having seen my look of concern. I had already noticed that the skin of her face was creased and almost orange in shade and that her voice, usually so forceful, had a tremor in it.

'I'm sorry to trouble you about something. I'll leave it for another time.'

'Please!'

'No, no. It's not important. It can wait. When you're better...'

'No, no. Tell me. But first – sit please.' The voice had recovered its commanding strength. She pointed to the straight-backed chair in front of the fireplace. Gingerly I sat down on it.

I all at once noticed that, even on that steaming day, she had a rug over her knees and was wearing a thick winter kimono.

'Yes?' she prompted.

Hesitantly I told her my trivial errand.

'I'm sorry, very sorry.' She said it as though she were apologising for some serious dereliction. 'We must do something of course. At once.' She called out for the maid, who shuffled in. She looked in hardly better shape than her mistress. Her ankles were swollen, as were her fingers, and there was a sty on the upper lid of her left eye.

They talked for a while in Japanese. Then Mrs Kawasaki turned her head up to me. 'She will call Otani-san. He does many jobs for me. Good. Honest. Please be patient.'

She put her head back on the pillows. She closed her eyes. I realised that I was being dismissed with her usual combination of decisiveness and courtesy.

'I hope you'll be better soon.'

She smiled and put a hand to her chest. 'Old. My heart is old.' Then a thought came to her. Did I like the Noh theatre? I shook my head. I'd never been to a Noh play, I told her.

'I think you'll enjoy it. Most foreigners don't, but with you I have hopes.' Again she summoned the maid and rapped out what I guessed to be an order. The maid stumped off, eventually to return with a pale-blue envelope with Japanese characters handwritten on it in darker blue. 'These are some tickets. For you and your wife. I can't go. I want to go but...' She rarely made a gesture but now she made one, extending her arms, the sleeves of her kimono falling back from them to reveal how emaciated they were, and at the same time shrugged

'Tell me what you think of our Noh. Be frank!'

⌒

'So what did she say?'

'She's going to get someone to come over.'

'Soon, I hope. Mark can't go on sleeping in that room with water dripping on to his head.'

I wanted to say, 'It's not dripping on to his head. It's dripping into the bucket that Joy placed on the carpet beside the cot.' But I decided not to do so. When Laura was in such moods of exasperation and despair I found it better to be silent. Instead I said, 'She gave me some tickets for the Noh theatre. It's for the day after tomorrow. You'll come, won't you?'

'Oh, God. Do you really expect me to go? Everyone says what a shattering bore it is. Worse than Kabuki.' Only a few days before we had gone to the Kabuki theatre. After it, Laura said that, had we not been the Ansons' guests, she would have walked out.

'Oh, do come with me! If you don't like it, you don't have to stay. It could be interesting.'

'*Interesting*! Are you crazy? No, no, you go but don't expect me to go with you.' She stooped over Mark in his cot, and then turned:

'How about your Miss Morita? Why not take her?'

'Because I'd so much rather take you.'

'Really?'

'Really.'

'No bloody chance.'

I rang Miss Morita later, when Laura had gone out for a walk with Mark in his pram. It was her mother who answered the phone. Having little English, she kept repeating 'Go out! Go out!' in mounting exasperation until I gave up without leaving a message.

I was working up in my tower room when I heard footsteps on the stairs. I knew at once that they were Laura's, just as Smoky, so many years later, always knew that it was my footsteps mounting the front-door steps of the house. I turned, half apprehensive and half pleased.

'Sorry. Sorry.' She stood in the doorway, hands clasped before her and head lowered, as though she were a schoolgirl appearing before her headmistress.

'Sorry for what?'

'Oh, for being so snappish about the Noh. I'd really like to go with you.'

'Really?'

'Really and truly. It might cheer me up.'

'I doubt it. Kyogen is cheerful – that's the farce – but the kind of Noh that we're going to see never is. It's all death, ghosts, love thwarted, children lost, that kind of thing.'

'Never mind. I want to go with you.'

⌒

The unrelenting rain pattered on our umbrellas as we scrambled out of the Cadillac and made a dash for the theatre. I was wearing what I called my outsize French letter, a light-blue plastic mackintosh that Laura hated. Her bare legs were spattered with water; my once light-brown suede shoes were dark with it and squeaked as I walked in them.

The audience was sparse. Between the high stage and the

54

unraked wooden seats under their canvas canopy, the rain was a shimmering screen through which one peered at the hieratic figures up above one on the stage. The play was Kenzo Motomasa's *Sumidagawa*. Since this was years before Benjamin Britten's *Curlew River* made the story familiar in the West, I was totally ignorant of it. I had brought with me a clumsy English translation, made by an obscure Japanese scholar and locally printed. Miss Morita had lent it to me. The combination of reading the text in the subaqueous light diffused through the falling rain, and at the same watching and listening to the actors was as difficult as nowadays coping with both surtitles and what is transpiring on stage at the opera.

With difficulty I followed the story. A crazed woman travels what is then a vast distance from Kyoto to the banks of the Sumidagawa River near Tokyo, in search of her lost son. The boatman who ferries her across the river gives her the shattering news, vouchsafed to him in a vision, that her son is dead. On the opposite bank a group of Buddhist votaries are chanting a prayer on behalf of the dead child. Mad with anguish, the mother joins them, banging wildly on a drum while she joins in their prayer. Suddenly the ghost of the child appears and then no less suddenly disappears as dawn begins to break.

From time to time I glanced sideways at Laura, fearing that at any moment, exasperated, she would jump to her feet and hurry off. But leaning forward in her seat, she was rapt. On two occasions I attempted to share the text with her, edging it towards her knees, but each time she pushed it aside. When the play ended, I rose to my feet. She remained seated, still staring at the stage. She moved her head a fraction so that a light above us caught her cheekbone. It glistened. Unconscious of my gaze, she raised a hand and with it wiped her cheek. I realised that she had been crying. I was astonished. How had she been able, without even a glance at the English text, to recognise the pathos of a piece of which she had previously known nothing and of which she had been able to understand not a single word?

All she would stay as we stepped out into the teeming rain was, 'Well, that got to me. It really got to me.'

Had that remote, highly formalised drama prompted in her a prescience of what was so soon to follow?

# (13)

I have come to hate the bloated, red-faced boor opposite. I have also come to hate myself for hating him. He has a jocular way of baiting an old toff like me but he is never hostile and often, in his crude, clumsy way, he even tries to be friendly. I ought to feel sorry for him, afflicted, to his patent embarrassment, with what he mysteriously calls 'one of those women's things'. (I shrink from pressing him to tell me what that can be.) Occasionally I do feel sorry for him, but there is always this unyielding substratum of hate, hate, hate. The fact that, as I watch him across the aisle, it is with my little eye as though through a telescope, only gives a sharper focus and intensity to my hate.

As I brood on his awfulness, Laura is suddenly clicking her way towards me. This is her second visit today. The post, always late now, had not arrived when she made her visit this morning and so she decided that she would bring it now. I am moved both by the frequency with which she appears beside my bed – suddenly there since, unless my head is turned, my little eye does not take in her approach – and by her obvious concern for me. This concern drives her to interrogate the nurses and even, on one occasion, Dr Szymanovski's Scottish assistant, who happened to be hurrying past. I suspect that the staff think and even say among themselves, 'Oh, that woman again!' They are all, as they often complain, rushed off their feet.

Today it is a large packet of letters that she removes from her bag. She looks unusually pale and, as she takes a step towards me, holding it out, her limp is so pronounced that I think for a panicky moment that she is going to fall. 'I've removed what seems to be junk. Lots of bills. I've dealt with those. I thought you'd want to see the letter from Joe.' Instead of handing it to me, she now begins to shuffle the pack as she looks for the airmail envelope that bears Joe's meticulous, minute writing of our address.

'Read it now if you like.'

'Later.'

In saying that, I have disappointed her. There has never been any urgency in my interest in Joe, any more than there has been any in his interest in me. From the beginning I tried to love him with the protective ferocity with which I loved Mark. But I could never achieve that.

'He's always so busy.'

She is making excuses for him. Since my stroke, he has telephoned once to ask how I am, and there has been a get-well card signed by him, his wife and one of their three daughters, the youngest, still living with them in Auckland. I met that daughter first as a child, when they brought her with them on a holiday visit to England, and then again as an awkward, enthusiastic teenager, when Laura had persuaded me that we must travel on to New Zealand after she had accompanied me to Australia on a lecture tour.

'Yes. It's extraordinary that someone should devote so much of his time to linguistics, of all things.'

'Is that any more extraordinary than devoting so much of one's time to Japanese art?' For all our years together, more than half a century now, her constant complaint has been that she 'just can't *get*' Japanese art. Once she even remarked of it, 'You always say that it's a miracle of less meaning more. But as far as I'm concerned it's a catastrophe of less meaning even less.'

I take her hand, in one of those sudden surges of love, a wave that sweeps in and then withdraws, leaving a cavernous darkness, that has, so puzzlingly to me and no doubt also to her, always characterised our relationship. 'I can see you've been doing too much again. You look tired.'

'Oh, it's that bloody boiler. So many telephone calls, so many excuses. I wish we'd never taken out that contract. It's almost three weeks since the whole problem started.'

It is she who has always dealt with the practicalities of our life together.

Abruptly I break out, 'I do wish that this bloody trouble with my sight would clear!'

'It won't. You know it won't. They've told you it won't. It's tough, but there it is. You'll just have to adapt yourself.'

*It's tough.* You're tough, I think. But I admire her for her refusal ever to embrace an illusion or to encourage others to do so. Far more than most people, she will begin a sentence with 'We've just got to face it.' Now I just have to face it.

When she says goodbye, leaning over to kiss me on one cheek and then the other, I put out my hands and pull her towards me. She all but topples over on top of me. 'Oh, I do wish I were out of here. With you. Back home.'

'It won't be long. Be patient.' She runs fingers through my sparse, grey hair. 'I'll come by tomorrow morning. But a little later than usual. That bloody plumber is coming at ten. *If* he comes.' She moves off, raising a hand in farewell. Then she turns. 'What about Smoky?'

'Smoky?'

'The ghost of Smoky. Is she still visiting?'

'From time to time. Not as faithfully as you do.'

As I speak, summoned as though by our talk of her, a grey shadow scuttles soundlessly across the ward and vanishes. I stare after it but say nothing.

I pick up Joe's letter and slit open the envelope with a knife forgotten by one of the two Polish sisters when she took away my tray.

The letter begins 'My Dear Dad.' I hate that 'Dad'. It used to be 'Daddy' and I hated that too. They have all, he writes, been so shocked and anxious since hearing the news of my stroke. It must be ghastly for me, with that restriction of vision, but it's good news that I can write and read with no difficulty and can even watch television. He had so much wanted to fly over at once to be with me but unfortunately, with the examination season upon them, that was out of the question. Rosie would have come, in fact had almost done so, but in the end she had so much wanted to see her boyfriend row in his eight at the annual college regatta that, reluctantly and guiltily, she had given up on the idea. Erwin took his rowing so seriously and so she too had to take it seriously...

Like all my letters to him, all his letters to me attempt to convey an abundance of love and concern when really there is little of either of those things. From the beginning, we mysteriously never really bonded, just as he and Laura never really bonded. Once, when I was reprimanding him, then only eight years old, for some trivial lapse in table manners, he had wailed, with an extraordinary passion, almost in tears, 'You want me to be Mark. But I'm not Mark. I can't be Mark. I don't want to be Mark.'

Stricken, Laura jumped up from the table and rushed round to put her arms about him. He shrank, as though she were about to slap him. 'We don't want you to be Mark, darling. We want you to be yourself. We love you as yourself.'

But she was lying. And the recalcitrant, despairing, unattractive boy knew that she was lying, as I did.

I cannot go on reading his letter, just as years ago I could not go on listening to him holding forth in wearisome periphrases and labyrinthine sentences each time that he returned home from Oxford for the vacation. I push it into the drawer of my bedside table. Tomorrow morning I'll read it, I tell myself. I might even try to answer between the tests scheduled for me.

Now, I want a snooze.

# (14)

Miss Morita laid out on the table the map that she had taken out of her bag. 'It is rather difficult to find,' she told us. 'Out of the way. First we drive to Hôrinji – well-known Shinto shrine. From there we go to Matsuno-o Shrine.' With a forefinger, the cuticle ragged around the nail, she traced the route on the map over which all three of us had bowed our heads. 'We do not visit shrine today. But later we must visit for the famous Rice Planting Festival. July twenty-three,' she added with her extraordinarily exact memory for such details. 'Saihôji is south-west of Matsuno-o Shrine.' Again she pointed. 'Here. The garden of the temple is famous all over the world. Now many people call it not Saihôji but Kokedera. Kokedera means Moss Temple. This garden is famous for moss – many kinds of moss, hundreds. This is the best time to visit, rainy season.'

Without my noticing Laura had drifted away from us. Arms akimbo, she was staring out of the window at the rain. She often stared out like that, transfixed by its relentlessness. She turned. 'It's raining. Always this bloody rain.'

'That's why it's called the rainy season. Let's make the best of it.'

'You must see Kokedera in rainy season,' Miss Morita intervened. When most people say that you must see this or that, it is no more than a recommendation. But when Miss Morita said it, the words, though uttered in a voice of cotton-wool softness and deadness, nonetheless carried an inflexible authority.

Laura moved away from the window. 'Oh, all right. Then let's get going.'

'Excuse me.' Miss Morita pointed at Laura's shoes. 'Such shoes are not good for Moss Temple. The moss is very damp, everywhere is damp.'

'Then I'd better change them, hadn't I?'

'That is good idea.'

As we threaded our way down a narrow, winding lane, and then bumped over an even narrower dirt track, branches rattling against the sides of the Cadillac and mud spattering not merely its body but from time to time even the windshield, Laura became increasingly exasperated.

'Are you sure we're going the right way?'

'Yes. Sure.'

'But it seemed so much shorter on the map.'

'In Japan every journey seems shorter on map.' Was Miss Morita merely stating a self-evident truth or was she being jocular? As so often, there was no way of knowing.

When I last visited Kokedera, during the rainy season almost half a century later, it was crowded with people wearing raincoats and carrying umbrellas. But fifty years ago it was totally empty, but for a tall, solitary man – a German, I guessed – in a long black, belted raincoat and a black homburg hat, a black umbrella held above him. He would from time to time place the umbrella, unfolded, on the ground beside him while he took yet another photograph with the Rolleiflex dangling round his neck. As we passed him, he nodded briefly at us, and I then said, 'Good morning.' I received no reply.

On our stepping out of the car, Laura struggled to open her dark green umbrella with its amber handle. It had once cost me a lot of money when I had bought it for her as a birthday present at James Smith. 'Please,' Miss Morita said. She took it from her and, with a small grimace, briskly unfurled it. She smiled and handed it back.

Laura said nothing.

The light was extraordinary, as though reflected off the moss stretching in all directions. Drops of water fell in heavy globules from the branches of the trees. Soundlessly the moss welcomed them. Miss Morita began to tell us about the priest Musô Kokushi who, in the twelfth – or was it the thirteenth? – century had designed it. 'A kind of male, Japanese Vita Sackville-West,' I said fatuously. I wished that she would keep quiet.

Suddenly Laura, who was walking a few steps ahead, no doubt in an effort not to have to listen to this lecture, turned and faced us. She lowered her open umbrella: 'I'm afraid I've had enough of this. I can't take any more rain and I can't take any more moss.' I half expected her to go on: 'And I can't take any more of these lectures.'

'But you must complete circuit,' Miss Morita protested. 'Everyone completes circuit. We have done only half. Please!'

Laura's only response was, 'I'll wait for you in the car.' She began to march back the way that we had come. Then, no doubt repenting of her rudeness, she turned: 'I'm sorry. So sorry. Don't pay any attention to me. Enjoy yourselves. I have a copy of *The Times* in the car. More than a week old but never mind.'

'She is making a mistake,' Miss Morita said, looking after her, head tilted to one side. 'I am sorry.'

'There's nothing for you to be sorry about. This incessant rain is getting her down.'

'Getting her down?'

'Depressing her. She hates it. But I love it,' I added.

'Maybe in a previous life you were Japanese man.' She said it as though she really believed that this might be possible. 'You understand us. We are different – and, like us, you are also different. Not like most Western men.' She shook her head. 'No, no. Not at all.'

I wanted silence, so that I could not merely hear the birds but also listen in vain for the sound of those globules of water falling endlessly down on to the iridescent moss. Fortunately, perhaps at last sensing this, Miss Morita stopped her endless chatter, as she stepped out beside me in her cumbersome, flat-heeled shoes – sensible shoes, my mother would have called them – a garish paper umbrella open above a grey felt hat with jauntily upturned brim.

Then all at once she halted and her hand shot out to my arm. She grasped it. 'Look!' she whispered. '*Look!*' She raised her umbrella with her other arm and pointed. 'Frog.' Underneath a cherry tree, its bole black with rain, I eventually discerned, screwing up my eyes, a small frog motionless but for a constant throbbing in its swollen throat. It seemed to be staring at us with eyes made of jet beads. Its body, like the bodies of those lizards that would now rest motionless in our boarding-house bedroom and now scuttle up its walls, seemed to be encrusted with emeralds.

We stood there looking at it for what must have been almost a minute. All that time her hand rested on my arm, and all that time I became increasingly conscious of it. The gentle pressure had an astonishingly disconcerting and yet also astonishingly transforming effect on me. I was not in the least excited or aroused by the contact, as I might have been from a similar contact with a woman sexually desirable, as Miss Morita certainly was not. But it transmitted to me a feeling of overwhelming tranquillity and, yes, at the same time of the joy that I have so rarely and so fleetingly felt in the course of my life.

The frog gave one leap, a second, a third, before vanishing from sight. I let out an involuntary gasp and realised that I had been holding my breath for several seconds before that.

Miss Morita removed her hand.

We walked on, once more in silence.

'Did I miss a lot?' Laura asked, as I opened the car door for Miss Morita to enter.

'Only more of the same. But that light – and that stillness! I've never experienced anything like it.'

Laura put a hand to the ignition. The engine thudded into life. The whole vast car shook, a prehistoric beast arousing itself from slumber.

# (15)

I am sealed in a tube. I might be a mummy.

'What sort of music would you like?' the handsome, tall woman with the thin lips asked me before I entered it.

'What can you offer?'

'Oh, almost anything.' She put her head on one side and surveyed me. 'You wouldn't opt for pop, would you? Jazz? Yes, you might opt for that. Or Gilbert and Sullivan. We have a nice CD of *The Mikado.*'

'No. Not that. Mozart perhaps?'

'Mozart it is.'

I lie listening to *Eine Kleine Nachtmusik.* I've heard it so often before, and now I've tired of its elegant, whimsical sweetness. It doesn't in any way distract me from my panic. Sealed with me inside the tube an invisible wild beast is emitting weird grunts, whirrings, and burps. The noises seem to be part of me, the symptoms of some violent digestive upset. I begin to count the seconds – no, not so fast, too fast, slower, slower! – to distract myself.

'Well, there you are! It wasn't so bad, was it?' Perhaps she says that to every patient that she imprisons in the tube. Perhaps she realised from the beginning how nervous I was.

'It was even worse than I'd expected.' I laugh. I want her to think that I'm joking. But I'm not.

It is not the usual effervescent, sweet-natured black porter (from Ghana, I have by now learned) who fetches me but an elderly man with sagging jowls and cheeks, who hums tonelessly to himself as he pushes the creaking wheelchair down the long, strangely empty corridor.

Suddenly he says, 'I wonder what we can expect now?'

I am puzzled. Is he referring to the result of the thallium scan that I've just endured? To my future health – or lack of it?

'How do you mean?'

'Well, there may be other explosions. I'd not be surprised. That's why we're on red alert.'

'Red alert? I don't get you.'

Suddenly galvanised out of his lethargy, he tells me the news. While I was imprisoned in my tube and that handsome, tall woman with the thin lips was monitoring its progress, three bombs had exploded in London. At any moment casualties might arrive.

Even the most moribund people in the ward are excited. They are all now staring up at the individual television sets above their heads, from time to time swivelling round to make some comment to a neighbour.

The red-faced, pot-bellied man whom I so much hate suddenly announces to everyone, 'They were bloody fools ever to let them into this country. Enoch Powell was right. Rivers of blood. That's what he said was coming. Too bloody right he was. We should boot the whole bloody lot of them back where they came from.'

I pick up my copy of *The Tales of Genji*, already read twice, in an effort to escape from a fizzing excitement that is as little to my taste as a tumbler of gaseous root beer.

As usual, Dr Szymanovski is already with me before my little eye has detected his approach. 'I'm sorry to have to ask this of you. But you've just had your last test and so it's not really essential for you to remain here. We can always bring you back in an ambulance when we want to monitor you.' I am puzzled. What's all this about? Then it comes to me. Why have I been so slow and obtuse? 'We haven't yet had to take in any casualties of the bombings. But we might have to – any moment now. The thing is we have to clear this ward – and some other wards. I'm sorry. Would you very much mind...?'

So far from minding, I feel a surge of relief, as though I were a death row prisoner suddenly brought his reprieve.

'Yes, that's fine.' And it is fine. 'Shall I get up and dress now?'

He nods. 'The sooner, the better. But take your time. No immediate hurry.'

I inch out of bed and open my locker for the clothes that have been getting more and more creased as the days have passed. I pull out a vest, and with it the trousers of my dark-blue suit fall out on to the floor. I stoop. Suddenly I feel giddy.

My blood pressure must have suddenly slumped, a side effect of my battery of pills. I lie back on the bed, the vest in one hand.

I twist my head round and look at the red-faced booby opposite. Dr Szymanovski is standing over him. I can't hear everything that he is saying, but it must be similar to what he has said to me.

Then I hear the booby all too clearly as he shouts in disgust, 'Bloody hell! I'm bloody ill!'

With a strange hyperaesthesia I can hear every word of Dr Szymanovski's cold, disgusted reply, 'I think that many of the casualties are likely to be iller than you are.'

'Oh, OK, OK! Anything to oblige! Whatever you say, Doc!' Muttering to himself, his face flushed, he swings out of the bed legs alarmingly thin for a man of his bulk.

Down in the crowded atrium of the hospital I wait for Laura, whom I managed to get on her mobile while she was walking in the park. Because there is nowhere to sit, I lean against a wall. I am still feeling dizzy. An ashen-faced, middle-aged man in a tattered dressing gown, leaning beside me, asks, 'Do you think it's OK if I smoke a fag? It might revive me.' He has already told me that a mate of his is coming to fetch him.

'I've no objection. But I don't know about the authorities.'

He lights up. Cupping the cigarette in his palm, he draws heavily on it three or four times and then begins to cough. A porter hurries over.

'Sorry, sir! Sorry! Strictly *verboten!*' He wags a finger.

'I can hardly go and stand outside.'

'Well, then I'm afraid... Sorry, sir. Regulations.'

The old man flings down the cigarette on to the marble floor and lunges out to stamp on it, with the same ferocity that Laura used to bring to her stamping on the cockroaches back in Japan.

# (16)

All those years ago the road out to Lake Biwa was not a crowded thoroughfare with constant traffic jams. Few people other than the rich had private cars, and buses, other than long-distant ones, were infrequent. Our journey was therefore leisurely and peaceful, with Mark asleep beside me in the back, and Miss Morita, beside Laura in front, mercifully breaking the silence only to sneeze violently into a lace-fringed handkerchief kept constantly at the ready in one hand, and to exclaim, 'Sorry, sorry!' She always had hay fever at this time of year, she had explained to us.

When we reached the lake, sunlight was slanting across it from above the mountains. Every sparkle stabbed at my eyes. In the hurry of our departure, I had foolishly, unlike Laura and Miss Morita, forgotten to bring my sunglasses. Now, when I complained of the glare, Miss Morita at once pulled off hers and offered them to me. I refused. 'Please, please! I do not need them,' she insisted. Eventually I gave in. Because they were too small for me, I had to wear them tilted uncomfortably at an angle.

Laura and I decided to swim at once. When we asked Miss Morita if she would be joining us, she put her hand over her mouth and began to giggle, as at the same time she violently shook her head. 'No, no! Never! I will stay with baby.' We might have been asking her to do something tempting but disreputable. A French couple, seated at a nearby table of the lakeside cafe to which Miss Morita had steered us – Laura had wanted a different, more isolated one – had already offered to look after Mark. Since they also had a baby in a carrier cot, we should have preferred to leave Mark with them. But Miss Morita was already lifting his cot to place it on a chair next to hers. She put her face close to his and half-sang what sounded like 'Ting-ting-ting! Ting-ting-ting!' Mark let out a scream.

'Do you think that she'll be all right with him?' Laura asked as, side by side, we entered the water.

'Yes, of course. She's very responsible. I just hope this water will be all right.' It was warm and slimy as I waded farther into it.

'Miss Morita said it was quite OK. And that Frenchman swam in it.' She looked about her. 'And there are other bathers.'

'Very few.'

Laura, a poor swimmer, floated near to the shore. I swam out and out, with an exhilarating sense of freedom. There was a rowing boat in the middle of the lake, with two men fishing from it. Its insubstantial image floated double, totally motionless above and below the still water. I thought that I might make that my destination but then gave up. I had not swum for two or three years and my arms, back and neck had suddenly begun to ache. Mrs Kawasaki had once told me that her son had planned to build a pool in the garden of the house, but that then the war had broken out and he had gone off to do his military service. Now that, the rainy season over, the weather was inexorably hotting up day by day, I wished that his plan had not failed to come to fruition.

As I began to dry myself vigorously, I realised that Miss Morita, seated with one hand placed on the edge of the cot as though to assert her possession, was squinting at me, her eyes screwed up because of her insistence that I should take her dark glasses. She leaned forward, both hands now clasped between her knees. 'You are an athlete.'

Laura laughed derisively. 'That's something he certainly is not. He's a weedy intellectual.' Later she told me, 'I wanted to add that the only sort of athlete that you were was a sexual one.'

Miss Morita clapped both hands over her mouth and was convulsed by one sneeze and then another. 'Excuse me! Sorry! Very sorry!' she cried out. Having dabbed at her nose with a handkerchief pulled from a pocket, she went on, 'Dr Anson has a copy of a statue of Greek athlete. It is called Discobulus. A little like you, I think.'

Laura again laughed, even more derisively. 'If he were to pick up a discus, he'd probably fall over with the weight of it.'

I felt miffed but said nothing. In sympathy, Miss Morita

sought my gaze and then gave what was clearly intended as a comforting smile.

All at once, usually so undemanding, Mark began to bellow.

'Oh, hell. I'd better feed him.' Laura turned to me. 'Where did you put the bag?'

'In the shade. Over there.'

Miss Morita at once leapt to her feet to fetch it.

The sushi and the tempura that we had ordered to follow it were both excellent. It was rare in those days to drink sake other than warmed. But on our behalf Miss Morita had insisted to the waiter that we should have ours chilled, even though she had previously admonished us that, to enjoy it at its best, warming was essential.

Suddenly Laura cried out in horror, 'What are you doing?'

Daintily holding a ball of rice from the sushi between her thumb and forefinger, Miss Morita was feeding it to Mark. She looked up startled. 'Sushi is fine for a baby. No problem. In Japan –'

'I don't care what is fine in Japan. It would certainly not be fine in England. Do please, *please* stop feeding him. Please don't give him anything, anything at all. I've already given him his baby food. That's enough.'

Miss Morita hung her head. 'Sorry. I am very sorry. In Japan –'

'Yes, I know, I know! In Japan, yes. But not anywhere else in the world.'

'Sorry.'

By the time that we had finished our lunch, the sun was low, a huge orange disc just above the serrated crest of a mountain to the west.

I jumped to my feet. 'I need a walk after all that food.'

'And I need a zizz.'

I began to walk away. Then I heard from behind me: 'I am coming. I am coming with you. Wait! Please wait!'

I halted, frowning. Behind Miss Morita I could see Laura. Her head was back against the chair, her straw hat tilted so far forward that most of her face was invisible. Her bare legs were stretched out ahead of her. Too short and with muscular calves, they were her one physical feature that I never found attractive. When, on our arrival, the three of us had walked together down to the cafe by the lakeshore, I had thought, with the surprise of a first discovery, how beautiful Miss Morita's legs were in comparison.

'Maybe you do not know why this lake is called Biwa. This lake is shaped like a *biwa*, a musical instrument maybe like your lute. Did you know – it is a little larger than the Lake Geneva in Switzerland? A volcano made the lake – some say in a single night. Maybe? Some say no...'

Remorselessly she went on and on. But, as I watched a small tourist steamer making what was, as Miss Morita now interrupted her lecture to tell me, a circuit of the 'famous' (her word) Eight Views of the lake, I found that I had become no more aware of that quiet, insistent voice than of the increasing whirr and thump from a factory – processor of dried fish, Miss Morita had broken off to tell me – in a crook of the wayward shore.

As we approached Laura on our return, she gave a little grunt, jerked up, opened her eyes, and stared at us as though not recognising who we were. She pushed up her hat, revealing a red line on her glistening forehead. 'Oh, there you are!' After a look at her watch, she added crossly, 'You've been gone an age.'

'Sorry. Miss Morita wanted to show me one of the eight famous views and we had to walk longer than I had imagined.'

'What was the view?'

'I think it's called "Sails Returning to Yabase". Am I right, Miss Morita?'

'Yes. Yes, that is right.'

'Unfortunately there were no sails. But Yabase was there. Very beautiful.'

'Sorry. But this is not the season for that view. We will come another time.'

'That'll be a treat to look forward to.' Laura scratched at a leg. Then she looked down and gave a little scream. 'Oh, my God, look at my legs! Look at these bites. What *are* they?'

'Mosquitoes, I think,' Miss Morita said indifferently. 'Such bites are common in the summer by the lake. Maybe you should have put on cream – or worn stockings.'

'Mosquitoes! Oh, my God! Do you think they can give me malaria?' Laura jumped up and peered into the cot.

'In Japan we do not have malaria,' Miss Morita said firmly.

'Thank God they didn't get at Mark.' Laura straightened. Then she stooped again, and, even more frenziedly than before, scratched and scratched. A bead of blood slowly swelled and began to darken where her long nails had lacerated the skin.

'My mother always say that best cure for mosquito bites is to soak with Japanese green tea. I am not sure. She say that tea must be specially strong.'

Laura paid no attention. She began to gather up her belongings.

'We haven't yet paid,' I reminded her.

She sighed. Then she held out her bag. 'Pay. There should be lots of money in there. I went to the bank yesterday.'

I paid and returned.

'You drive!' Laura held out the keys to me.

'Really? You always say that it's more tiring to sit in a car in which I'm driving than to drive yourself.'

'Do I? Well, I don't feel that today. This heat seems to have drained me of all energy.'

'It is not so hot here as in Kyoto,' Miss Morita interjected. 'Many people come to Lake Biwa to be cool.'

'That suggests that they can't be very bright.' Laura, who was carrying the cot with Mark in it, indicated the rear door beside her with the toe of her shoe. 'Open that, would you? I'll go in the back with Mark and you can go in front with Miss Morita.'

'But I can go in the back with Mark-chan, no problem,' Miss Morita protested.

'I think it'll be best if I'm with him.'

'As you wish.'

Having seated herself, Miss Morita pulled off her straw hat and rested it on her knees. She sighed in contentment. Her hair, damp with sweat, was stuck, like the tendrils of a creeper, to her wide forehead, 'On the way home we can stop at Ishiyama.' She turned to me. 'Maybe you know that Ishiyama is famous for its Ishiyamadera Temple – Stony Hill in English. In the temple there is a building called Genji-no-ma. You have heard of it?' She turned her head to address Laura, who made no reply. 'You know of course of *Genji Monogatari – Tales of Genji*?'

When Laura made no response, I put in, 'Oh, yes, of course

71

we do. There's a wonderful English translation by someone called Arthur Waley.'

'The author is Murasaki Shikibu. She was born nine-seven-five, I think, and died maybe ten-thirty-one, ten-thirty-two. She write her famous book at the temple. Soon we make detour. I will tell you.'

'No. I'm sorry, Miss Morita. We must leave that detour for another time. I think that I must get Mark home.' At that Laura broke off to exclaim, 'Oh, hell! He's been sick all over me.'

I glanced over my shoulder – something always hazardous, however brief the glance, if I am driving. Mark's face looked grey against her sunburned arm. Puke glistened momentarily on his chin, until Laura briskly wiped it away with a handkerchief. I turned back to the road ahead.

Then I heard: 'It was that sushi! He's too young for rice. I knew, knew that it would only upset him!'

In consternation Miss Morita wailed, 'Oh, I am sorry, sorry, sorry! But in Japan we think that for baby –'

'I don't care what you think in Japan. Please, please never feed him anything.' There was silence. Then Laura added, 'Ever, ever again.'

When, having left Miss Morita off at her mother's house, we were getting out of the car, Laura, who was still inside, lifted the cot to pass it to me, standing by the open rear door.

'Oh, Christ! He's done it again. More rice from that wretched sushi. What an idiot that woman is. One can only hope she never has a baby of her own.'

The next day the bead of blood on her leg had become a scab. The day after that the scab was surrounded by an inflamed ridge of tissue. On the third day she was running a temperature.

# (17)

It's strange. The house seems smaller, darker and damper than before and, when I get into my bed this evening – Laura and I no longer share a bed or even a bedroom because of my insomnia – the sheets are clammy. I do not mention this to Laura because I know that my grumbles always upset her. 'Why don't you take a more positive attitude to things?' is a question she often asks.

There is a bottle of champagne on ice to celebrate my homecoming before we sit down to an early dinner of smoked salmon, filet steak and salad, and the kind of chocolate soufflé that she makes to perfection. As she pours me a second glass of the champagne I don't remind her that Dr Szymanovski told me that while I was on warfarin I should never drink more than one glass of wine at each meal. He had added, shaking a finger at me, 'And no binge drinking! No binge drinking!' I had replied, 'People of my age don't go in for binges,' and he had then forced a laugh.

'It's wonderful to have you back.' She extends a hand across the dining table and places it over mine. 'So much sooner than I'd expected.'

'It's wonderful to be back.'

'Some tiny good comes out of even the most terrible things.'

'Should we be drinking champagne when so many people have been killed and mutilated?'

'If the killing and mutilation of people meant that no one drank champagne, then all the champagne firms would go bankrupt.'

For the next few days she is extraordinarily protective of me.

'Are you sure you can find your own way up the stairs?'

'Yes, of course I can!'

Later: 'Would you like me to cut up that steak for you?'

Later still, when I am peering into my handkerchief drawer: 'I'd better look one out for you.'

Eventually, I say, 'Oh, please! I'm not blind, you know. My

sight has just become restricted. It's inconvenient but not a tragedy.'

'Sorry. Yes, I looked tunnel vision up on the Internet. In the States someone has invented some sort of lens that can compensate for the loss.'

I remain silent. I have already wearied of visitors to my hospital bedside telling me of lenses, specialists, or quacks that might be able to 'help' or even cure my partial loss of sight. I must, as Dr Szymanovski has more than once told me, merely try to adapt myself to the handicap, as people adapt to the amputation of an arm or a leg.

Lying awake in the grey light of dawn, I think that I can see a darker shape at the bottom of my bed. With a strange mingling of dread and elation, I think: *Smoky*! Then, with a no less strange mingling of relief and loss, I realise that it is only the dressing gown that I dropped there, instead of, as in the past, hanging it up on the hook on the door.

When eventually I drag myself out of bed, I cannot find my glasses. With my tunnel vision the task of hunting for even an object so large often takes an age. I jerk my head from side to side and up and down in growing frustration. The glasses ought to be on my bedside table but they are not. They might be on the dressing table but – no. Then at long last I see that they are resting on the top of my computer. Why on earth should I have placed them there? It is not even as though I had used the computer since my return.

In the same way I find myself hunting for the key to the puzzle of why for so much of the time – putting down a book or a newspaper, switching off the wireless or the CD player, ceasing to listen to what people are saying to me – the memories of events in those few months in Japan almost half a century ago should now obscure and even crowd out ones that were once so much more vivid. Freakishly the tunnel vision of my mind keeps insisting on focusing on them to the exclusion of everything else.

# (18)

Laura found the summer even less tolerable than the rainy season before it.

Fretfully, almost venomously, she cried out to me from the bed on which she was lying, at midday, in only a flimsy nightdress, 'Oh, do try to get hold of an air conditioning unit for at least this room!' Air conditioning units, now ubiquitous in Japan, were then a rarity.

'You mean buy one?'

'What else could I mean? Steal one?'

'Well, rent one. That must be possible.'

'No, buy one, buy one!'

She was still on the antibiotics that Dr Anson had prescribed for the septic mosquito bite, after he had lanced it – a procedure that Laura had endured in silence, with the same stoicism with which, having refused an injection at the dentist, she endures the resulting pain. 'She certainly has guts, your lady,' he said, as I was seeing him out, Joy hovering – if anyone so large could be said to hover – behind us. She had, unasked, been present at the lancing, soundlessly wincing, as though in pantomime, each time that Laura had done so.

Despite the lancing and despite the antibiotics, it was as though the septic bite had introduced a poison, insidious and potentially deadly, into Laura's system.

Endlessly and, as I saw it, needlessly she worried about Mark. Obsessively she weighed him, to announce despairingly that he was not putting on the weight that he should. When, many years later, Joe would burp up food or void a foul-smelling diarrhoea into his nappies, it worried her not at all. But when Mark did so, she would become almost hysterical.

'Oh, that stupid, stupid woman! Why the hell did she have to force that muck on to him?'

'She never forced it on to him. She offered it to him.'

'Crazy! It was probably off. I don't image the hygiene in a restaurant of that kind would be anything to boast about.'

'We all ate the sushi. Far more than he did. He never had more than a tiny mouthful. He must have sicked up most of that in the car. We've had no ill effects.'

But it was useless to reason with her.

Increasingly she would remain in our air-conditioned bedroom, drooping on a wicker chaise longue or lying out on the bed, her face often pressed into the pillow. The cot, with Mark in it, would be beside her. Joy would come and go, bringing and fetching trays of food or the iced lemon barley water that Laura had come to prefer to any other drink. She would now often address Laura as dear or even darling. Her usually strident voice would become hushed, as though she were entering a sickroom. Perhaps it was a sickroom, I often thought. Could Laura be having what people called a nervous breakdown? I had never been sure precisely what that term implied.

After Dr Anson, a brisk, cheerful man with a painfully aggressive handshake, had returned to ensure that the infection from the mosquito bite had totally cleared up, I took him down from the bedroom not to the front door but to the sitting room.

'You know, I'm worried about my wife.'

'Oh, you've no cause for that. Not now. The wound has almost healed.'

'I don't mean that. The problem is that she's always been so full of energy and now, suddenly, she seems to have none at all. She spends most of the time upstairs in that bedroom.'

'Well, it does have air conditioning.' At that he pulled out a handkerchief and began to mop his forehead. I had already seen the beads of sweat clustered, like small blisters, on it. There were also dark patches of sweat under the arms of his generously cut seersucker jacket. 'I wish we had a unit in our bedroom up at the mission. There's been talk of installing some units since last summer and now we're in the middle of this one. I don't think you have anything to worry about. People not used to this kind of damp heat often react badly to it.' Again he pulled out the handkerchief and mopped his forehead, so briskly this time that he might have been attempting to scrub off a stain. 'Well, I must be on my way. Thank goodness we have air conditioning in our operating theatre. I have three operations scheduled for just this morning and it's now' – he glanced at his watch – 'oh gosh, almost eleven.'

⌒

All at once – paradoxically on a day hotter and more humid that any we had so far experienced – Laura took a turn for the better. Having jumped out of our bed a little before six, she hurriedly pulled on some slacks and a blouse, slipped her feet into a pair of rope-soled sandals bought in the local market only a few weeks before, and left me, still half-asleep, to race down the stairs. Before long I heard noises from the garden. I staggered out of bed and crossed to the window. She was working out there, vigorously tugging at rampant weeds and then tossing them by the handful into a wheelbarrow. My first emotion was one of anger. What was the point of paying the elderly gardener whom Mrs Kawasaki also employed, if Laura took on one of the most onerous of his tasks? But then I was relieved. This was the Laura that I knew – energetic, purposeful, amazingly quick and proficient at anything to which she set her hand.

Later I heard Joy's voice. She must have just arrived on her bicycle, as she always did at this early hour, to prepare our breakfast. We had repeatedly told her that, since what we liked was so simple – coffee, toast, butter, marmalade, a banana or an apple – there was no need for her to get it for us. But she had insisted that she was only too happy to perform this task, and had then added that in any case she could never sleep late. She ended by bringing out her often uttered, 'No problem, no problem.'

'Do you think that you should be doing this heavy work, dear?' she now asked. 'I was shocked when I saw you.'

Laura's laugh was clear and untroubled. 'It makes me feel terrific. You know, back in London I'm the one who looks after our garden. Of course it's no more than a handkerchief –'

'A handkerchief?' The way she said it, I at once thought of Lady Bracknell. It was odd that the use of the word should puzzle her.

'Very, very small. But gardening is something that has never interested my husband. If I ever go away without him he even forgets to water the pot-plants.'

I let the curtain drop and flung myself back on to the bed.

The icy blast from the air conditioner played full on my body, naked from the waist up.

Later that day Laura said, 'Why don't we go to see that Kurosawa film? Everyone's talking about it – even, believe it or not, the Shotts.'

I was amazed and delighted. For days now I had proposed outings to her – to visit this or that temple, to go to Nara, an expedition still not undertaken, to accept an offer from Dr Anson to show us round the hospital – and each time she had refused. Fretfully she would always give the same reason: it was so hot, hot, hot. It was even too hot, she would insist, either for the game of cribbage with which, in the past, we had so often passed a vacant evening, or for the sex in which we had until only recently taken so much pleasure.

Since, although she knew hardly any Japanese, she had none-theless responded with so much emotion to the Noh play, I thought that she would have no problem with the film. But as soon as we had entered the virtually deserted cinema, she once again became snappish and fidgety. The seats to which we had been shown were far too near the front, she complained, and so we moved farther to the back. But as soon as she had sat down there, she sighed, 'Oh, this seat is hopelessly uncomfortable. It sags in the middle.' We moved again. Then, in the middle of the trailer, she started to complain about the quality of the sound – it was just *awful*, couldn't I hear the crackling? When the film itself had started, things were no better. She sighed deeply, examined her fingernails, turned her head to look all around her, crossed and uncrossed her legs, coughed noisily and at one moment even began to hum under her breath.

Increasingly exasperated, I eventually flung myself round to her, 'You're not enjoying this.'

'How right you are! It's a bloody bore. How can he ever have got his reputation?'

'Well, it did win the Grand Prix at the Venice Film Festival.'

'That figures. Only something so pretentious could do so.'

I returned to the film, trying to concentrate.

Another sigh. Then a groan. Then, 'I'm off.' She got to her feet.

I watched her as she strode towards the exit. Reluctantly and angrily I decided that I had better leave too. Out in the daylight

I hurried to catch her up. I grabbed her arm and pulled her round. 'Wait a moment!'

'You didn't have to follow me. I know that that sort of arty crap always knocks you over.'

I was astonished. She had never herself been a philistine. It was she who had forced me to go twice to *Endgame*, at a time when I used to dismiss Beckett as pretentious, ludicrous and a bore. But I decided not to argue.

Instead I asked, 'What would you like to do now? The last time I saw her Mrs Kawasaki recommended a restaurant called Inaho. One of the best in Kyoto, she said, and unlike most best restaurants, not all that expensive. It's ages since we ate out.'

'Do you think it has air conditioning?'

'I doubt it. If you want air conditioning we'd better go to the Miyako Hotel.'

'What I'd really like to do is try one of those sake joints of which one is always reading in Japanese novels.'

'Do you really want to go to one? Their clientele is usually male – the only females are on the staff.'

'Well, that's an added incentive. You know that I always prefer the company of men.'

'Professor Takahashi' – this was one of my academic contacts at Kyoto University – 'took me to one in Gion. I think I can remember where it is. That was the occasion when he got so drunk that he almost toppled into one of the canals as we walked home.'

Suddenly her mood changed, as though a lowering, black cloud had all at once shredded and disintegrated. She linked her arm in mine. 'This is going to be far more fun than watching that dreary *Sanjuro*. It's so long since we went out together.'

I saw a telephone box. 'Do you think we'd better give the Shotts a ring to make sure that Mark is all right?'

Those days, when Mark was not with her, Laura would become morbidly anxious. But now, to my surprise, she at once waved aside my suggestion. 'No, I don't think so. They're so good with him. The only trouble of having them is that that pipe of his always makes the whole house stink.'

The bar was wide open to the alley, its sliding doors pushed back. But some short, gaudy curtains, billowing now in and now out as a fan rotated in front of a vast cube of ice set out on a tin tray, made it virtually impossible to see the customers, perched on their stools, except from their waists down. Most of them were in summer kimono, with wooden *geta* on their feet.

I pushed up a curtain and we entered. All heads turned. The man behind the bar, a cloth tied round his head to look like a makeshift turban, greeted us. I returned the greeting. There was a single stool vacant at either end, but no two stools next to each together. We were about to withdraw, when an elderly man staggered to his feet, gave us a tentative smile and moved along to the stool most distant from us. The waiter pointed to the two stools now empty beside each other: '*Dozo, sensei.*'

Laura clambered on to her stool. 'This is fun – even though I'm the only woman here. Do you think they mind?'

'They'd probably mind if you were a Japanese woman. But since you're a *gaijin*... We *gaijin* are a different species. The rules of the Japanese species don't apply to ours.' The waiter had set out two sake cups and now waited, flask in hand. 'Hold out your cup. You must hold it out when he pours out for you.'

She held out the cup. Sitting to the left of her was a middle-aged man in a creased blue pinstripe suit and a white shirt open at his scraggy chicken-neck. His scarlet face had a dazed but happy expression. It was clear that he was drunk.

Suddenly he turned his head and, in a blurred voice, announced to Laura, 'In Japan we have rule. Sake cup must never be full, sake cup must never be empty. You understand? All time he' – he pointed at the waiter – 'fill glass. All time you' – he pointed at her – 'empty.' He tittered. 'So – everyone happy.'

The fleshy young man with tattooed forearms on my right, his bristles of cropped hair glistening with oil, now leaned across me to ask Laura, 'You English?'

'No. I'm American. My husband is English.'

'Good. Very good.' At that he once more lapsed into a morose silence, resting his chin on a hand and staring into space.

'I'm really rather enjoying this.' After two small cups of the sake Laura already seemed to be tipsy. She turned to the man in the shabby suit who had first spoken to her. 'Do you come here often?'

He drew in his breath, as though the question were a tricky one, and his head rocked from side to side. 'Sah!' Then he nodded, 'Yes. Often. After work I come here. Have good time.' He raised his cup. 'Cheerio!'

'Cheerio!'

I might not have been there.

Eagerly Laura began to ask the man a whole succession of increasingly intimate questions. He answered with more and more reluctance, taking in a gulp of air each time before he did so and draining his cup of sake as soon as he had finished. Soon, I realised, everyone in the bar was listening to these exchanges, even though I guessed that few of them were capable of following them. I wished that Laura would stop. Her present euphoria was now disturbing me as much as her increasingly frequent periods of depression and lethargy in the past few days had ever done.

Suddenly, in peremptory fashion, she banged on the counter with her cup. 'More! More, please.' She held out the cup. The waiter poured, with deliberate slowness. He was staring at her with a gaze that suddenly struck me as disapproving, disgusted, even hostile. 'Arigato!' It was one of the few Japanese words that she knew. She raised the glass and sipped. 'To you, old chum!' Ignoring the toast, he turned away, stooped and fetched a metal tray from under the counter. Banging one hand on it, as though it were a tambourine, he then disappeared into the back of the bar.

'How about a move?'

'Oh, no. I told you – I'm having fun.' She gulped again at the sake. 'Lots of fun.'

It was at that moment that I realised that the whole atmosphere had changed. Our fellow drinkers, their faces all flushed, had ceased to find our intrusion either amusing or interesting. So silent previously, each lost in a private world of dazed contentment, they were now suddenly all talking to each other, their voices growing more and more strident. No doubt they were habitués and so, long-time acquaintances. There were giggles, then explosions of laughter. The eyes that had once glanced at us only momentarily had become confrontational in the derisive, even aggressive, fixity of their gaze. I slid off my stool and asked for the bill. The waiter, instead of producing

one, merely muttered a sum. I was too confused to grasp what
it was and so held out some notes for him to take what was
owed. Carefully he selected what he wanted. Then, without a
word, he turned away.

'We don't want to leave now,' Laura protested.

'Yes, we do. Come on. *Come!*' I grabbed her arm above the
elbow and jerked her off her stool.

'But why –?'

'Come!'

Outside she turned on me angrily, 'What got into you?'

'They wanted us out.'

'What are you talking about? They were so friendly.'

'Not at the end. That's their world, not ours. They wanted us
out.'

'Rubbish!'

'I could understand only a little of what they were saying but
I can tell you – it wasn't friendly.'

'Oh, you imagine these things. You get so paranoid.'

'*Me* paranoid?' I put a hand on her shoulder. 'Shall we take a
little walk? It's pleasantly cool now.'

'Yes, why not?' Her mood had again changed with disconcerting abruptness. 'But can you remember where we left the
Caddie?'

'I think so, hope so.'

Miraculously no longer tipsy, she took my arm in hers and
rested her head on my shoulder. 'I'm so glad we left that awful
film. That was such an amusing time in that bar. I loved that
little man in his business suit. Priceless. Thank you for taking
me there.'

⤙

As we approached the house down the long lane, we saw that
there was an ambulance at its far end.

Laura was horrified. 'Is that ambulance outside our house?'

'I don't think so. Why should it be?'

'Perhaps something has happened to Mark.'

As we neared, the ambulance took off. We then glimpsed the
Shotts standing together on the pavement, not outside our
house but outside Mrs Kawasaki's.

Laura jumped out of the car, leaving the door open. 'What's
happened? What's happened?'

Mrs Shott trotted over and put a hand on her arm. 'Don't worry, dear. Mark's all right. It's Mrs Kawasaki. That maid came over in a terrible state to say she'd had a turn. So we called an ambulance.'

'A turn? What sort of turn?' But there was now none of the previous shock and anxiety in Laura's voice, merely interest.

'We don't know,' Shott took up. 'It seems she must have passed out.'

'She was conscious by the time that they carried her out to the ambulance. On a stretcher. She even saw us and recognised us.'

'She sort of smiled.'

'The maid's gone with her.'

Far off I heard the pipe, with its three mournful notes, of the late-night noodle man with his stall on wheels. Students, swotting into the early hours, were his chief customers.

'How about some noodles?' Laura suddenly suggested. 'I love those noodles of his.' She turned to the Shotts. 'You could do with some, couldn't you?' She had, it was clear, already forgotten Mrs Kawasaki now on her way to the hospital in an ambulance.

'Well, I don't know...' Shott was dubious, 'It's getting kinda late.'

'Just for a short while.'

'OK. If you insist.'

'Darling' – Laura turned to me – 'get us four bowls. I'll warm some sake. I've drunk a lot already but I could do with some more.'

# (19)

I still marvel at Laura's patience and care. This morning she insists on bringing my breakfast to me in bed. Then she runs my bath, supports me on the short walk along the corridor to the bathroom, and insists on helping me in. She picks up my facecloth. 'Let me soap you.'

I laugh, at once touched and irritated. 'I'm not an invalid. I can do it for myself. I really can.'

'That young Scottish doctor told me that you must take things easy.'

'Taking things easy doesn't mean not doing anything for myself.'

As I get out of the bath, she watches me, a towel at the ready. Then she envelops me in it and begins to rub me vigorously. Later it is with difficulty that I stop her from kneeling down and pulling on my socks for me.

Dressed, I tell her that I want to walk down to the local library to consult Laurence P. Roberts's *A Dictionary of Japanese Art*. She at once stops emptying the dishwasher and insists that she will come with me. I protest that that is totally unnecessary but she is already pulling on a coat.

'No, you don't have to guide me. Just warn me if I'm about to walk into a lamp post or a dustbin. Or someone else.' In fact I am feeling nervous and exposed. I should like to clutch on to her but know that I mustn't. As Dr Szymanovski keeps impressing on me, I must learn to adapt.

In the reference section I open the book and turn to the entry that I want. I am seated, she looks over my shoulder. 'Shall I read it for you? That print is so small.'

Patiently I explain to her, as I have repeatedly explained to her in the past and as I have had to explain to so many other people: 'There is nothing wrong with my central vision. With my glasses it was always fine for reading, it's still fine. What I've lost is my peripheral vision. That's nothing to do with my eyes. It's to do with an area of my brain.'

'Don't you want to take the lift?' At her insistence we took it on the way up to the reference section.

'No. I must get used to stairs.'

She frowns and then steps away from me. But she is close to me, a protective guardian, as we walk down. 'Hold on to the rail. Firmly. The last thing you want is a fall.'

I'm tempted to say, 'The first thing I want is for you to stop fussing over me.' But with difficulty I restrain myself.

When, out in the street, she takes my arm, I jerk away. 'No! Let me manage for myself. Please.'

'Oh, you're so obstinate!'

Now I am sitting in the conservatory that we added to our little Queen Anne house three years ago. I am in the reclining chair into which, arm around my shoulders, she insisted on helping me. A new biography of Yukio Mishima rests on my knees. When I have finished reading it – if I ever do – I'll post it to Miss Morita. Since his death, at once so shocking, so preposterous and so futile, she has been weirdly obsessed with him. When she has referred to him in one of her letters, as she frequently does, I make no mention of him in my replies.

I look out into the garden and watch Laura, the summer sun glinting on the thick white hair that she now wears in a straight pageboy bob. She is cutting some roses. The snip-snip-snip of the secateurs sounds as if she were shredding the air.

This morning I have been increasingly exasperated by her solicitude for me, and I have tried less and less to conceal that feeling. But now, seeing her absorbed in her task, I feel simultaneously moved, abashed and guilty. When in Kyoto all those years ago she suffered that near-breakdown, I constantly tried to pretend both to her and, worse, to myself that nothing was amiss. If she wanted to lie for hours on end in our air-conditioned bedroom, while I visited yet another temple, garden or palace, well, that was her choice. Yet here she is, half a century later, repaying that indifference with so much concern, kindness, pity and, yes, love.

She comes through the door, the roses in one hand. I suddenly realise how beautiful she still is. The lined face is perfect in its symmetry, the cheekbones far more pronounced, the eyebrows far more strongly chiselled, and the mouth far more firm than during that long-ago period of excessive heat, turmoil and unhappiness.

I am about to get up from the chair. Swiftly she puts the roses down on a table.

'Wait! Let me help you. Wait, *wait!*'

Reluctantly, the exasperation surging up in me like a corrosive bile, I wait.

# (20)

Laura had moved the cumbersome air conditioner close to her chair. Or, since it was so heavy, perhaps Joy had moved it for her. Mark was in a crook of her arm, motionless, eyes fixed unwinking on me as I approached. At that moment, with his smooth, shiny porcelain skin and his strangely red lips, he fully deserved Mrs Shott's repeated reference to him as 'A doll! A real little doll!' He really might have been one. The breeze from the whirring machine raised the fine, blonde hairs, little more than fluff, on his scalp.

Laura did not even raise her eyes when I said, 'Hello, darling. How are you feeling?'

'Hot.'

'But it's really quite cool in here. In my study it's almost unbearable. That fan does no good at all. I tried to work for a while but I couldn't.'

'I keep changing my clothes. I can't stand the stickiness.'

I suddenly remembered a fellow student at Oxford, with whom briefly I thought myself in love. With the same obsessiveness with which Laura would now change her clothes, sometimes three or four times a day, this student would constantly scrub her hands, so that they had the raw appearance of having recently been scalded.

'How is he today?'

'Well, he hasn't been sick since the last feed. But his weight isn't right. Dr Anson said there was nothing to worry about but what does he know? He's not a paediatrician, he's primarily a surgeon.'

'Would you like me to ask Mrs Kawasaki for the name of a paediatrician?' The old woman had recently returned, emaciated, unsteady and shaken with tremors, from the hospital.

'Oh, God, no! Better a second-rate American surgeon than some Japanese witch doctor.'

I went over and placed my hand gently on Mark's head. I felt a terrible sorrow. There was something so defenceless and so pitiable about him, as he looked up at me with his bemused, wondering, pale-blue eyes, edged with almost white lashes. Gently she edged him further up the crook of her arm, as though deliberately to remove him from my touch.

'I was wondering. Would you like to come to this party with me?'

'*This* party? What party is that?'

'I told you. Katinka's birthday. We don't have to stay too long. I've bought her a box of Marazoff chocolates as a present. Far more expensive than she deserves but there it is.'

Slowly she shook her head, while with a chiming slowness the fingers of her right hand now lifted and now patted Mark's near-white fuzz of hair. In a considered tone she said, 'I don't like that woman. Not at all. Why should I help to celebrate her birthday?'

'She's not all that bad. She was kind to us – on balance. When I run into her in the street –'

'When I run into her in the street I try to make myself scarce before she can see me.'

'You don't have to talk to her. We'll see some of the people we met while we were – '

'My, what a treat!'

I ignored the venomous interruption. 'And I gather from the Shotts that there are some interesting new ones.'

'The Shotts are the sort of people who find the *Japan Times* so interesting that they spend a whole day reading it. Oh, please!'

I continued to try to persuade her but soon realised that it was hopeless.

'Well, you won't mind if I go, will you? For a short time.'

'Why should I mind?'

'Remember, it's Joy's day off.'

'I'm not likely to forget. Without her...'

She broke off.

'Yes? Without her?' It was ridiculous to feel these sudden jabs of jealousy over someone so ugly, whose only talent was for cooking and cleaning.

'I don't know how I'd survive.'

'Are things really as bad as that?'

She turned her head away. Mark let out a little mew as she shifted in the chair. She said nothing.

↝

Garish paper streamers sagged from a ceiling that was still, as I remembered from our brief stay, yellow-grey with grime. On a square lace cloth on a round table in the centre of the room, two vases of towering, ponderously scented lilies flanked a portrait of Katinka, clearly taken at least twenty years before, in an elaborate silver frame. At its base was a card bearing the words in ungainly capitals:

DEAREST KATINKA
SEVENTY GLORIOUS YEARS
HAPPY BIRTHDAY

A rosebud was drawn inexpertly with pink and green crayons on one corner. Nudging the card out of position, was a wrapped present, thin and long – an umbrella? a stick? – and a bulging brown paper bag presumably containing another present. There were also presents behind the card, on either side of it, and on the floor. I added my box of chocolates, in the used gift paper that Joy had found in a drawer before impatiently relieving me of the task of clumsily wrapping it up.

I looked around for Katinka. Then she emerged through the door from the kitchen. She was bearing a large oval Pyrex dish, piled high with sausage rolls, in gloved hands. Having set down this load on one of the two long tables, next to a platter containing an even higher-piled load of thickly cut sandwiches, she hurried over to me, arms outstretched and calling out my name.

'Those sausage rolls are a present from your Joy. You tell her of birthday? She is so kind a lady. I invite her but she has other job.' Strangely, while wrapping my present, Joy had said not a word to me either of her own present or of the invitation. 'Once she works for me – long time ago.' She looked around her and then asked, 'But where is your lady?'

'Oh, my lady sends her best wishes and apologies. She's not all that well ... This heat is getting her down.'

Katinka rubbed hands twisted with arthritis down her dirndl skirt as though to tame its extravagant, multi-coloured flounces. The nails, many of them chipped, had been varnished bright red and for the first time I was seeing her lips not pale and chapped, as they usually were even in the summer furnace of that time, but crimson with lipstick, a smear of which had somehow got on to one side of her chin. 'Oh, I am sorry. Joy told me something.'

Before I could ask what the something was, Katinka's husband, his feet in their usual slippers, shuffled by bearing a tray on which filled glasses rattled, in danger of toppling over. Since he did not stop for me, I reached out and tried to grab one.

'Not champagne,' Katinka warned. 'Too expensive. A cup. A little this, a little that, a little' – she turned her face up to me with an impish smile – 'something secret, very secret, known only to Katinka. If you prefer – Coca-Cola, of course.' She reached out for a half-empty bottle of Coca-Cola from a nearby table, either anticipating my choice or making it for me.

I shook my head, as she held the bottle out to me. Did she expect me to drink from it? I knew that the Coca-Cola would be the highly sweetened version manufactured in Japan. I hurried over to Katinka's husband, now some distance away, and seized a glass of the cup. I sipped. The taste, both bitter and saccharine, was oddly similar to that of marmalade. 'I've left our little present on the table with the others,' I told Katinka.

'Oh, you are so kind. Always so kind. You know, this is special occasion, not ordinary, not at all. Today I top seventy. So much happen in my life, revolution, one husband die, then China, then Japan, then war, then children – all everywhere now, not here, some in States, some Australia, one Mexico. And here I am, landlady – with no money! I feel I am a hundred.'

'You don't look it,' I volunteered.

She closed her right hand into a fist and punched me with it on the chest, hard enough to make me gasp. 'You maybe flatter.'

How right she was!

Rex from the British Council was pushing himself through the crowd, followed by a young Japanese. 'You must meet my houseboy. I brought him along because he loves this sort of social occasion. Don't you, Masa?' The boy grinned. 'He's on the Doshisha American football team. Aren't you, Masa?' The boy grinned again.

Through the open French doors I could see the Shotts

standing, each the centre of a group, in the narrow backyard. In one corner there were three dustbins, one with its lid lying upwards beside it. In the other corner two bicycles rested, shackled to each other, against a peeling wall. Shott was smoking his pipe.

Seeing me, Mrs Shott beckoned frantically and then called out, 'Come and join us!'

I made my excuses to Rex and walked over to her.

'I want to ask you – what news of your neighbour?'

'Again in hospital.'

'*Again*? That looks bad.'

'There's talk of her son coming back from Brazil.'

'I don't like the sound of that. He's a medic, isn't he?'

'A famous one, I gather.'

'Well, perhaps he can do something. Though I have a feeling – things having gone so far – and considering her age...'

At that moment Shott shouted to me, 'Stop flirting with my wife and come over here for a sec! I want you to meet a young lady, just arrived, from your country. She's a painter, believe it or not. But not in the line that interests you. She wants to work with some folk called the' – he turned to the girl standing in front of him, her back to me – 'what are they called, dear?'

'The Gutai group.'

'Have you heard of them?' he asked me.

'I'm afraid not.'

In a deep, husky voice with a trace of West Country accent, the girl said, 'No reason why you should. But they're going to be famous.'

'And you're going to become famous along with them.' Shott put a hand on her shoulder. 'Now, Betty – that is your name isn't it? – I know you'll get on fine with this fine English gentleman. He knows a lot about painting – Japanese painting.' The hand went from her shoulder to mine, as he propelled the fine English gentleman closer to her.

There were freckles across the bridge of her nose and on the chest exposed in a vee where her blouse had two of its pearl buttons undone. Her eyes were green, with sandy lashes, and her forehead was low under a widow's peak of thick, auburn hair. She was not a beauty, far from it. But immediately I felt as though a spark had ignited the dead wood of the days of boredom, unease and sexual frustration caused by Laura's seemingly unstoppable drift into indifference and despair.

As so often in such situations, I spoke too fast, while at the same time fumbling for words. She appeared to be interested in me, but perhaps that was just a social adroitness. She could not have been more than in her early twenties but she had about her an impressive air of competence and composure.

'I'd like to see your pictures.'

'Would you really? I doubt it.' She laughed with what I can only describe as spontaneous delight not merely in our conversation but also in her new life in this odd boarding house in this even odder country. 'So far I've only painted one since I arrived here. I've been so busy settling in and adjusting myself. All my other pictures are back in England.'

'Are you liking it here?'

'Oh, yes, of course, yes, yes.'

'And the heat? That doesn't bother you?'

'Oh, no, I love it! I don't want to sleep. Every night I go out for a walk along the canal. It's so calm, so beautiful.' She broke off. Her face had suddenly lit up as, now on tiptoe, she peered over my shoulder. 'Oh, there's my new friend! We met two days ago. He's teaching at a university called Ritsumeikan.' She waved an arm frantically. Then without a word, she left us and rushed back into the dining room.

'Well, that's a sweet kid,' Shott said. 'Now I must propose madam's health. Excuse me.'

I did not wait for this. As all the other people in the yard began to crowd into the dining room, I looked for an immediate exit and found it from the yard into a narrow passage, crammed with litter and dead leaves, and so out into the road.

The fire that the girl had ignited in me still crackled away, at once disturbing and exhilarating. After we had been for so long so sexually active, Laura's and my relationship had deteriorated into no more than a friendship, sometimes affectionate but for the most part scratchy and querulous. During the past days the heat that had made Laura so apathetic had made me increasingly horny. I had begun to masturbate – something that I had rarely done since my schooldays – two or three times each day. But the satisfaction was similar to that which I had experienced for a brief period during which, as an undergraduate, I had been a chain smoker. For a few minutes the hunger was appeased; then it reiterated its demand even more urgently than before.

On my journey to the party, I had not brought the car but instead had walked up from the lane and along a narrow pathway that provided a short cut, through a wasteland in which people exercised dogs that they always kept on leads, up to the boarding house. Now I took the longer route along the canal. That was the route that she – that girl, that Betty – had told me she took for her evening walks, alone in the past but perhaps soon with the man with the shoulder-length hair and the face so oddly wizened for someone of his age, to whom she had waved so excitedly and who had eventually waved back with what appeared to be no more than amused condescension.

Walking through the falling dusk I was lost in a fantasy. I had wandered out for a stroll along the canal. She was leaning over one of the little, arched wooden bridges. I came up behind her so stealthily that she did not hear me. 'Betty.' She swivelled round. She cried out with pleasure. 'You!' Now we were seated side by side on a bank, its grass yellow-brown because of the unseasonable drought of the last few days, staring at the glimmering water in silence. I placed a hand on the back of her neck. I moved it round and down. I inserted it into her *broderie anglaise* blouse and cupped one of the small, uptilted breasts that I had all but glimpsed below its deep vee. I circled a nipple with a forefinger. She gave a little sigh and upturned her head ...

The barking of a dog snapped the delicately spun thread of this reverie. A tiny man in kimono and wooden clogs was straining to restrain a huge German shepherd that, I suddenly realised in a moment of panic, was making, upreared on the end of his chain and baring its fangs, for *me*. The man peered through thick granny glasses while still struggling with the dog. 'Sorry! Sorry!' Suddenly the dog became placid, even friendly. It wagged its tail, and then snuffled at something squashed and black – a bird? a rat? a turd? – lying in the middle of the path beside me. 'Sorry,' the man repeated.

↶

After the intensity of the heat outside even at dusk, the air-conditioned bedroom seemed glacial. Although it was only a few minutes past nine, Laura was asleep. Mark was also asleep in his cot, both fists tightly clenched as though to steel himself for some ordeal. On a table there rested the tray on which Joy had presumably set out a cold supper for Laura before leaving for home on her old-fashioned bicycle, with its high, wing-like handlebars, that made her sit so imposingly erect.

I began to take off my sweat-saturated clothes, dropping them at random to the floor instead of placing them carefully over the back of a chair. As I did so, I felt the mounting insistence of an erection. I approached the bed, then halted. I sniffed under one armpit, then the other. I turned away and made for the huge, high-ceilinged bathroom with its once white but now cracked and murky tiles covering every wall. I took the bottle of Caron down from the shelf above the washbasin and splashed some on to myself. I now associated its scent with making love to Laura. As that scent entered my nostrils and then coiled, snake-like, through my whole being, my desire for her intensified to such a degree that I all but ran back to the bedroom. For a moment I stared down at her. Then I jerked back the sheet that covered her naked body.

She stirred briefly as I lay for a few seconds against her, spoon-fashion, right hand to one of her breasts. As I lifted my left arm and moved my left hand up between her legs from behind, she jerked away from me, and rolled over to the far end of the double bed that she was always saying we must have replaced since it sagged so much. Then she sat up.

'Stop! *Stop*! What the hell are you doing?' Her hair was tousled, her eyes squinted with extraordinary malevolence.

'Oh, come on. Come on.'

'*No!*'

'But look – it's an age – '

'Oh, for Christ's sake!' She glared at me. 'And you *stink!*'

I thought that she was complaining of sweat. But then she went on, 'Why do you have to splash that awful stuff all over you? I loathe it.'

# (21)

She holds out the sweater for my inspection.

'I've never finished anything so quickly. When you were in hospital, I worked incessantly on it – except when I visited you.'

There is a harsh, metallic blue thread glinting from it. With sinking heart I know already that I do not like it and that I will wear it only to make her happy.

'When you were away, I didn't seem to want to do any of the usual things – read, go the cinema, see friends. I didn't even want to go to the shops and you know how I usually love to do that. I missed you, you know.' She stares at me over the top of the sweater with suddenly woebegone eyes. 'If you were to go first, I really think I'd make an end of it all.'

'What are you talking about? Don't be stupid.'

She nods emphatically.

'Anyway Dr Szymanovski told me that there was no reason why I shouldn't go on living for years and years. There are all these new drugs that I'm on – six different ones.'

'Yes, I've bought you a special dispenser for them. So we can be certain you take them regularly. I'm going to sort that out in a moment.'

'You think of everything.' Once again this thinking of everything both wearies me and fills me with gratitude.

'Try it on! Come on!'

She shakes the sweater at me and I take it from her. I know already that, even apart from that metallic blue, there is going to be something else wrong with it. I slip one arm into it and then struggle to slip in the other.

'Shall I help you?'

'No, no, I'm perfectly capable of...' I go over to the pier glass and survey myself. My cheeks have sunken in and have a shiny, grey look. My eyes seem unnaturally large. My hair, sticking up in thin wisps, needs cutting. The sweater is far too long. It reaches almost to my knees.

I turn to her. 'Wonderful!'

'You don't think it's too long?'

'No, no. Of course not. I don't like sweaters short. They make me look even more pear-shaped than I am.'

'Sure?'

'Absolutely sure!'

I go over to her and kiss her gently, fleetingly on the mouth. 'You spoil me, you know. You always have done.'

Like an over-exacting, over-strict parent, I have never spoiled her.

# (22)

Miss Morita, in a white linen suit that I had not seen before and the straw hat with the jauntily uptilted brim that I had seen all too often, had called for me. Joy left her standing in the open doorway as she came to tell me, 'That Japanese lady is here.' She said it in a grimly disapproving voice. She knew Miss Morita's name perfectly well, having met her over at Mrs Kawasaki's even before our arrival in the house and having seen her so often since, but when she spoke of her it was always 'that Japanese lady'. I had begun to wonder whether the frequency with which I was seeing Miss Morita had convinced her that we must be having an affair.

I went out into the hall. 'Oh, there you are! You're early, aren't you?'

'Sorry.' She hung her head, contrite.

'Nothing to be sorry for. I was just struggling with an article that's already begun to bore me and will probably bore any editor to whom I submit it.'

'I don't think anything that you write can be boring.' There was a note of reprimand in her voice. 'I am early because Mrs Kawasaki has not returned from hospital. When I visited her last night, she said that she would be home this morning. But now they must have decided to keep her. I rang and rang but no one came.'

'Oh, I hope that doesn't mean something serious. I really must go and see her.'

I had been saying that repeatedly. Nowadays I have, inevitably, become habituated to visiting sick and even dying friends as ancient as I am, but in those days even the disinfectant smell of a hospital filled me with dread and I shirked that duty. Laura, tougher and more conscientious, had already visited two or three times, as Mrs Kawasaki had been shuttled between hospital and home. But perhaps, if the car had not been air-conditioned, she too would have stayed away when the heat was so oppressive and she was constantly so lethargic and depressed.

'I am sure a visit will make her happy.'

'One moment.' I walked down the long, narrow corridor to the kitchen, from which I could now hear Laura and Joy talking together. When talking to Joy, Laura's voice sounded vigorous, interested and cheerful. It now rarely sounded like that when talking to me.

'Would you like to come with us?'

'Oh, no, not in the least.'

Swiftly I put a finger to my lips to shush her – as she so often did to shush me when Joy was in possible earshot. The rejection was so decisive that I feared that, if heard by Miss Morita, it might upset her.

'It's said to be the most extraordinary collection. Probably the finest in Japan. He's built it up over many, many years.'

'You know what I think of *ukiyo-e*. It's just poster art.'

I wanted to retort that that was a thoroughly stupid and ignorant thing to say. But, largely because Joy was present, turning her head from Laura to me and then back again, as though watching an aggressively contested game of table tennis, I managed to restrain myself.

'Oh, very well. But you're missing something. It's rare for him to show the collection to a stranger of no importance like me.'

'Well, I'll bear with that.'

As we drove down into the town, the icy blast of the air conditioner made Miss Morita hug herself in protection.

'I wish I knew how to adjust this wretched air conditioner. One either boils or one freezes.'

'It's fine. Please don't worry.'

She had the Japanese stoicism. 'Giggle and bear it' must be inscribed on every Japanese heart.

She began to tell me about the man whom we were about to visit. Mr Yamamoto was a businessman, with interests not merely in Japan but all over the world. His house was one of the oldest in the city. He also had an apartment in New York and a house in Paris. He talked little. Some people complained that he was rude. It was through a professor at Kyoto University, a friend both of his and of one of her cousins, that she had managed to get in touch with him to ask if he would show me his collection.

From its narrow frontage on a lane threading an area that looked like a slum, the thatched, outwardly dilapidated house looked far from impressive. A woman servant in kimono slid open the door to us, bowed and gestured to a row of slippers set out on the highly polished floor. As, clumsily, I tried to take off my laced shoes, I almost toppled over. The servant raised her hand to her mouth, stifling a titter. Then I sat down on the single step in front of me and removed them there.

For a long time, seated on cushions on the floor of a small, four-mat room, we waited. Then an elderly man, his short-sleeved, tie-less check shirt buttoned up to the neck and his too short grey linen trousers revealing bare, bony ankles, appeared soundlessly in the doorway. Miss Morita rose with practised elegance to her feet. I scrambled to mine. He was as unimposing as the frontage of his house.

After Miss Morita had introduced me, pointing to me with a hand held palm up, the fingers extended, as though she were proffering an invisible dish, Mr Yamamoto led us down a series of corridors so highly polished that at one moment my slippers skidded perilously. I soon realised, with amazement, how large the house was. From time to time, on left or right, one looked out on an exquisite little garden and heard from it the sounds of dripping water. The room at which we eventually arrived, at the end of the house farthest from the road, had an air conditioner in it. But, unlike the one that I had purchased, as noisy as our ancient refrigerator, this one was eerily silent.

He gestured to us to sit on either side of a low table. Then, with a tiny groan and an even tinier grimace, he lowered himself on to the cushion at its head.

Miss Morita began to translate – from time to time asking him, with head tilted in apology, to repeat something that she had failed at first to grasp. This, he began to explain, was the room in which he kept the best of his prints. There were a hundred – later Miss Morita told me that he had given the absolutely exact number – in this room. There were at least a thousand stored in other places.

What had first drawn him to the collecting of *ukiyo-e*? When Miss Morita translated my question, having until then been so remote, even chilly, he threw back his head and laughed, his mouth so wide open that I could see his uvula and the two gold crowns on adjoining back molars. Fishing, he replied. *Fishing?* He nodded his head, enjoying my amazement. Yes, fishing. From an early age it had been his greatest pleasure. It still was. Once he had visited an English business associate merely to salmon-fish on his Scottish estate. Fish, particularly carp, often appeared in *ukiyo-e*. Did I know that? They were symbols of vigour and long life. He was clearly now enjoying telling me all this. That was why they so often appeared in pornographic prints. He had many such, he added with a sly smile. His interest in fish had extended to an interest in the erotic scenes of which they were a small part.

He unlocked cupboard after cupboard and delicately set down print after print, each in its transparent wrapper, on the highly polished mahogany of the table before me. It made me uneasy that he watched me so closely, eager to see my reaction, each time that a print replaced its predecessor. Miss Morita peered over my shoulder – sometimes muttering something in Japanese, sometimes emitting a gasp or sigh of admiration. I'd nod my head. 'Beautiful.' He understood that word, and nodded each time when I brought it out.

A tall, dignified woman in a dark brown kimono appeared almost without a sound. She was carrying a tray, with three tumblers of iced tea on it. She bowed each time as she set them down before us. She bowed again in turn from the doorway before she left. Miss Morita was later to tell me that this woman was Yamamoto's wife. Her cousin had once pointed the couple out to her when they saw them in the distance in the Kabuki Theatre. 'Strange he didn't introduce his wife to us,' I remarked, to receive the answer, 'No, in Japan it is not strange.'

After Yamamoto had carefully replaced the last print set down on the table, we sipped our tea. He questioned me about my research and asked me whether I knew this or that foreign expert on Japanese art. In later years I was to encounter many of the people that he mentioned. Then I could merely shake my head in embarrassment or desperately say something like, 'Well, I did once meet him for a moment at a lecture he was giving.'

He jumped to his feet. Now he had a surprise for me, Miss Morita translated. Would I be interested in seeing some of the erotic prints? He was in no way embarrassed or hesitant in making this proposal. Nor, surprisingly, was Miss Morita. I shrugged. 'Why not? Yes.' Print succeeded print, with couples grimacing with effort as they neared a climax or lay back beatifically relaxed after they had attained it. Gravely he pointed out that the Japanese were the inventors of the close-up. See here – he pointed. Circled was a blow-up of a vagina. In another print the circle was around a cock magnified to the size of its owner's head. Looking over my shoulder, Miss Morita was decorously composed. There was none of the jocularity that an English equivalent of Mr Yamamoto would have displayed in a similar situation. At one point he indicated an area of a print in which, a woman, her body unnaturally twisted, was clenching both teeth and buttocks at the moment of orgasm. 'Beautiful.' He said the word, in English, in a way that made it clear that he was not sharing my sexual excitement at the image but was merely drawing attention to the perfection of the line and the subtlety of the colour.

When we were once more in the car, Miss Morita gazed down at the card that he had handed to her on our departure. 'He wishes you to have this. He likes you.'

'Oh, I was probably only a tiresome interruption in a long day.'

'No, no, he likes you. I am sure. That is why he gave me card for you. When he gave it, he said he wished see you again.' She held out the card and I took it. It was printed on one side in Japanese and on the other in English. 'When an important Japanese give you his card, he says, "Let us be friends."'

I laughed. 'It won't be easy to be friends with someone who speaks not a word of English.'

'I will translate!' She gave her usual laugh, always too shrill to be wholly attractive, her hand over her mouth. 'And you are learning Japanese.'

'Very slowly.'

'You must be patient. Japanese is difficult language. Very difficult.'

It was not the first time that she had told me that. Like most Japanese she derived pleasure from the belief that for a foreigner to learn to speak Japanese was an almost impossible task. Now that I have learned to speak it, I know the error of that view. To learn to write *kanji* is another matter.

# (23)

Laura is in slippers and dressing gown as she shuffles into the kitchen for breakfast. Usually she gets up before me, slips out of the bedroom to have her bath and then, fully dressed, prepares the breakfast to which she then summons me. Sometimes I am dressed, sometimes still in my pyjamas.

Now she rubs her forehead with the back of a hand and peers around her, as though unsure where she is. Her hair, usually so sleek and tidy, is a mess. There are grey shadows under her eyes.

'How did you sleep?'

'Badly. I had these dreams. I always do before today.' She goes to the toaster and inserts two slices. She looks around. 'Do you know what day it is?'

'Of course.'

'And it means nothing to you?'

'It means something to me,' I reply, trying to be gentle. 'But it doesn't mean as much to me as it means to you.'

'Well, no, that's obvious.'

'Today brings a memory. It brings a sadness, but so do most other days as well.' I am exasperated because on so many other anniversaries I've said this or something like it to her. 'I constantly think of him, constantly mourn for him. I don't set aside a single day to do those things. To think of him and to mourn for him is not like giving an Easter egg or filling a Christmas stocking. He's always here.' I raise a hand and tap my forehead with my forefinger. 'He's also always *here*.' Now I put my hand over my heart. There is no insincerity in the gestures even if they are so actorly.

The toaster pings as the two slices of bread shoot up. She reaches for the chopsticks beside the toaster and with them extracts, as she does every morning, the slices of toast still too hot to be handled. Slowly she sits down and stares at the slices on the plate before her, as though she had no idea what they were or why they were in front of her.

'No juice?' I hold up the carton.

She does not reply. She is staring out of the window. I lean forward, eager and apprehensive. Outside, beyond the smeared pane, I briefly glimpse, out of the corner of my little eye, a grey shadow whisking past. So, after so long, Smoky is back! To Laura she has been invisible, as always.

She turns towards me in a kind of bewildered panic. Then in a sad, soft voice she asks, 'Will we never get over it?'

'Too late now. It's become part of us. We've fed on the loss for so long. People become what they eat.'

She begins to cry, the sobs jerking out of her. I jump up, go round the table to her, and fold her in my arms. Her whole body is now shuddering violently, as though in a fit. She is retching on a grief that for all these years, more than half a century of them, her body still refuses to assimilate.

'He was such a beautiful child,' she gets out. 'How could that have happened? Oh, if only –'

She breaks off. I know what will follow.

'Oh, if only he had never gone to that nightmare country!'

'He could have picked up amoebic dysentery in all sorts of places.' I feel a deathly weariness. We have had this conversation so often before.

'Oh, don't be so idiotic! Not in England. Have you ever heard of a child picking up amoebic dysentery in England? Children may *die* of it here, when they have come from abroad. But they don't pick it up from being forced to eat stale sushi in a filthy Japanese restaurant.'

I want to argue with her that the sushi wasn't stale and that the restaurant wasn't filthy and that he might have as easily picked up the dysentery on the plane home or at one of its exotic stopovers. But I am silent. What would be the good?

I hold her tighter to me. That is all I can do.

# (24)

All that day Laura seemed, by some miracle, at last to have emerged from the shadows. She was out of bed long before I was. Half asleep, I was aware, with sudden refreshment of the spirit, that she was singing in the bathroom. She has, even now in old age, the voice of a musically gifted schoolgirl – small, accurate, silvery, fresh. She was singing that favourite air of hers, *Sakura*, then hugely popular and still hugely popular in Japan. Constantly hearing it in cafes, on the radio and even in the house as Joy crooned it in her deep, vibrant contralto while rocking Mark in her arms, I had begun to hate it for its sentimental sickliness. But now the distant sound of Laura's singing it to herself filled me with relief.

At breakfast she announced, 'It's a lovely day. We must get out.' Even her voice was buoyant.

I had still not completed the article on which I had been working for more than ten days. It bored me even more than ever, but I have a dogged persistence that prevents me from giving up on a task once I have started on it. I hesitated. Then any scruples were swept away by my delight that such a suggestion had come from her and not from me. 'Where would you like to go?'

'I leave it to you. Choose somewhere beautiful and exciting.'

'Well, how about Daitokuji? That's said to be both those things. People keep recommending it.'

'Perfect.'

'What about Mark?' I indicated him in his cot under the window. For once he was not screaming in what often seemed to me to be a combination of despair and baffled rage, but lying quietly asleep.

'Joy could look after him. She loves doing that.'

'No.' I nearly added: She spends far too much time with him. 'Let's take him with us.'

'D'you think that's a good idea – pushing him around in the chair? Unless of course you carry him on your back like a

104

Japanese mother – or like Brian Anson with that latest of theirs.'

'Oh, all right. Let's leave him.' I realised that all along I had not really wanted to have him with us.

'And let's also leave Miss Morita. Don't ask her to come with us, please, *please*! I don't want one of her lectures.' Her tone made me uncomfortable. Yes, she was teasing me; but, as so often with outwardly friendly teasing, there was a rancorous undertow.

I nodded. 'Agreed. No Miss Morita. Just ourselves. That's what I want.'

'That's what I want too.'

Daitokuji, we discovered, was not so much one temple but a cluster of them. For once it was I who found that my energies were flagging and Laura who insisted that we must press on and on. Soon, as morning veered to noon, the heat became intense. But amazingly, after all her previous complaints, Laura now seemed to be impervious, as she strode out, often ahead of me, Leica at the ready. It was wonderful to see her so totally and, as it seemed to me, miraculously revitalised.

We perched side by side, staring out at Soami's garden. 'I don't know which is the more beautiful, this or the other one.'

'You mean Enshu's? This, I think. Yes, I'm sure. This.'

She put her head on my shoulder. 'It's terrific to be here with you. Alone. No one else. Have you noticed how cool one feels here? It's not really cool, not if one looks at a thermometer, but one has this extraordinary illusion; everything cool, cool, cool.'

'Let's go and look at a few more of what the guidebook calls "priceless art objects". And then we'd better think of eating.' I glanced at my watch. 'Gosh! It's almost two.'

A solemn, silent, round-faced novice served us with many small dishes containing food often so difficult to identify that Laura and I would argue at length without ever agreeing precisely what it was. I longed for some sake. Instead I kept gulping at iced barley tea.

Later, as I put my hands on the steering wheel of the Cadillac, I let out an involuntary 'Ouch!' It was as hot to the touch as plates left too long in an oven. The leather of my seat was scorching my bottom through my crumpled cotton trousers.

Laura turned her head to me and smiled. It was a long time since she had smiled at me with so much joy and love.

'That was wonderful.'

'Yes, wonderful. There's so much to take in here. We'll never be able to see it all.'

'But we must try.'

The air conditioner, clattering and grinding away, was at last beginning to make a difference to the stifling temperature.

'Yes, we must come again. There's so much we haven't seen. Let's come again soon.'

I closed my eyes. For the first time for many days I felt totally happy and at peace.

'How has my little treasure been?' As Laura leant over the cot, her blonde hair screening her face, I suddenly experienced a violent, literally breath-taking upsurge of love for her. I drew the air deep into my lungs, once, twice. I had to touch her, now, at once, even though Joy was there on the other side of the cot, also looking down at the sleeping baby. I put a hand on her bare shoulder.

'Oh, he's been a marvel,' Joy was saying. 'Hardly a sound from him all day. He looks so much better, doesn't he? He's getting all his colour back. Right as rain.'

She would have gone on talking, but for once Laura cut her short. 'I'm afraid we're later than we said. I am so sorry. You'll want to get home at once.'

'Well... If that's all right with you, madam... I've left some corned beef hash for your dinner. In the refrigerator. You only have to warm it up. It won't take you more than a few minutes. And there's cheese and grapes.'

'Oh, thank you. That's fine. You're an angel.'

'If that's all right then... Are you sure you wouldn't like me to stop over to serve things up?'

'Oh, no, we can manage perfectly. Thank you so much.'

I felt that, such was her impatience, Laura was restraining herself from pushing Joy's substantial bulk to the door.

As soon as she had gone, Laura began to race up the stairs. 'Come! Quick! *Quick*! Not a moment to be lost!'

'But we have a whole evening of moments ahead us.'

I began to race up the stairs after her.

Now she lay like an exhausted athlete after a marathon. Eyes closed, hand, palm upward, concealing her face, and her body glistening with sweat, she gasped for breath with an occasional hiccupping sound. When I touched her, she pulled away with a grunt, so that she was on her side, cheek pressed into the pillow. Strands of hair stuck to her forehead. I lay motionless for a while, propped on an elbow, staring at her. I wanted to say to her, 'That was the best. Ever. The very best.' But there was something daunting in the distance that she had seemed all at once to have put between us after that period of frenzied closeness.

Eventually I scrambled off the bed and walked round to the table beside it. I pulled open its single drawer and extracted the packet of Camels that I kept there. Camels were her smoke, not mine. I also kept a lighter in the drawer.

'What are you doing?'

'Getting a ciggy.'

Always after we had had sex, there was what I called the 'postplay' of a cigarette passed back and forth between us.

'Must you?'

'No. But I'd like to.'

'The stink gets into everything. I hate it when I lie down at night and it's still there on the pillow and sheets.'

'All right. Never mind.' I pushed the cigarette back into its packet and dropped both packet and lighter back into the drawer. She and I were the least regular of smokers, lighting up from time to time after a meal or when waiting for someone or something. But I was addicted to that post-coital cigarette and felt exasperated at being cheated of it.

I lay down again on the bed. I stared up at the ceiling. Now, as at Katinka's, we had our lizards. This was a small one of an exceptionally vivid, luminous green. The sight of it somehow assuaged my disappointment and dismay. I put out a hand and touched her shoulder. I was about to say, 'Look at that lizard. Have you ever seen anything more perfect?' But she had already again moved away from me. Then she did a puzzling, disturbing thing. With a hand she brushed her shoulder vigorously where I had so briefly just had contact with it. She might have been brushing away a shower of dust or a cobweb.

After a few seconds I again scrambled off the bed. This time I walked down the warm, creaking bare floorboards to the bathroom. In my haste to make love to her I had forgotten to screw back the hexagonal black top of the bottle of Caron. I did so now. My fingers were trembling and I all but dropped it. The shower was gently dripping as it had been doing for days. I turned the cold tap to full and then clambered into the bath and stood under it. The water, always lukewarm from the cold tap during these summer days, hit my head and shoulders with a stunning force.

~

I was naked under my dressing gown. Laura was formally elegant in white silk trousers and a fuchsia silk jacket, both made for her, for an astonishingly small charge, by a dressmaker recommended by Mrs Kawasaki. She had also put on a pair of crocodile leather shoes made for her by Lobb's – the kind of extravagance in which she would so often capriciously indulge in those far-off days. She might have been about to go out to a party, instead of to eat corned beef hash in the kitchen with me.

'Hungry?'

She shook her head. 'Not really.'

'It's almost nine.' Like everyone in Japan, we usually ate our dinner far earlier than that.

She sighed and got to her feet. 'OK.'

From the tall, narrow refrigerator with the orange-yellow stains that Joy had tried in vain to remove with violent scrubbing, I took out the Pyrex dish containing the hash. I stared dubiously at it. I had always thought that one ate corned beef hash as soon as one had cooked it.

'Do you think it's all right?'

Impatiently she replied, 'I'm sure it is.' Then she added, as I carried the dish over to the ancient gas cooker, 'Oh, don't fuss so!'

I put the dish down on the kitchen table, preparatory to lighting the oven. But she forestalled me, taking a taper from where Joy kept them in a chipped tumbler and then lighting the taper with a match. She stooped, opened the oven door and turned on the tap.

As the oven ignited with its usual small pop, she let out a

piercing scream and reared away, lighted taper in hand. She went on screaming on the same high, piercing note as I rushed towards her. She pointed.

Later, in telling one of her many stories of the horrors of life in Japan, she would talk of 'a cascade' of cockroaches, an 'army' of them, and once, to everyone's amusement, a 'herd' of them, a slip for 'horde'. They plopped out of the oven on to the floor and then scuttled off in all directions.

I put my arms around her, pressing her tightly to me. At once she struggled to free herself. When I still held her, she gave me punch in the side with a fist. Then she yielded to me. Her body became limp. She began to sob. 'Oh, God, this country! This bloody country!'

⌒

'I can't eat anything after that.'

'Of course you can.'

She bit her lower lip. 'I can't go into that kitchen. Never, never again.'

'Don't be silly. You remember what Katinka told us – cockroaches are a way of life in Japan.'

'Stupid cow! Well, it's not a way of life I'm prepared to adopt.'

After we had retreated into the sitting room I had poured her a stiff gin and tonic. Now she held it out, wordlessly, for a refill.

'Do you really want another? Wouldn't it be better if we had some dinner? Not here, if you'd rather not. We could go to that little sushi place up the road.'

'*Sushi*! Not on your life!'

'Well, there's that restaurant opposite to it. People say it's OK. Nothing special, but OK.'

'Oh, all right. But I must have another drink first. We'll have to take Mark.'

'Yes, of course. It's not far to push him.'

Mark was a success with the elderly woman who waited on us. She spent so much time cooing and chattering to him in Japanese that it was a long time before she brought our simple order of chicken curry and rice. Laura, head supported on hand, hardly spoke. Soon I too lapsed into silence.

'There are too many flies in here,' she suddenly announced.

'There are too many flies everywhere in Japan at this time of year.' Suddenly I felt exasperated.

'Haven't they heard of fly papers?'

'Evidently not.'

When we walked out of the restaurant, pushing the pram together, it was into an exceptionally beautiful night. A strong breeze had arisen, causing the trees on either side of the lane to rustle and creak. I tilted my head backwards. The whole sky was crammed with stars, unbelievably many. Now Laura looked up. She was as dumbfounded as I was.

'I've never seen a sky like that.'

'Nor I.'

Our hands touched on the handle of the pram. Then she raised hers and put it over mine. I was astonished by how cold it felt. It seemed to me that, once again, she had emerged from another of her moods of extreme desperation.

The next morning Miss Morita arrived to take away some typing that I had set aside for her. She stood in the doorway of my eyrie while I searched for the sheets of paper and sorted them numerically. I have always been an untidy worker. Usually I'd have urged her to sit down – something that she would never have done on her own initiative. But now I deliberately refrained from doing so. I wanted to be free of her presence, so gentle and modest and yet so intrusive. For someone to demand more of a friendship than I am prepared to give always gets on my nerves.

'Thank you.' She gave her usual bow, little more than a slight inclination of the head. Her feet in their flat-heeled brogues were almost touching, her gaze was lowered. Then she looked up. There was a disconcerting pity in the wide-spaced eyes behind the gold-framed spectacles.

'Maybe I'll see you tomorrow?'

'Let's take a rain check. I'll call you. Or vice versa.'

'Rain check?'

'We'll see how things are going.'

She nodded. Then she had left, swiftly and silently.

After a few minutes the door opened again. It was Laura. She walked decisively to the chair opposite to my desk and sat down in it before speaking. 'I must talk to you.'

'Yes, of course.' I pushed the blotter with my work on it away from me. 'What is it?'

'I've come to a decision.'

I already knew, God knows how, precisely its nature. 'Yes?' I shifted in the chair. Suddenly I felt not merely a mental discomfort but also a physical one. There was an ache in my shoulders and my head seemed too heavy for my neck.

'He's had another upset. We can't let them go on.'

'Don't worry. I'll telephone Anson.'

'Later.' She leaned forward. 'Listen to me.'

'Yes? I'm listening.'

She tilted her head as though straining for a prompt inaudible to her. Then she said, 'I must go. He and I must go.'

'Go?' But I knew exactly what she intended.

'We must get out of this bloody country. Or it's going to kill us. Both of us.' She stared at me and I stared back. 'I don't know what you want to do.'

'I can hardly go now. My scholarship still has more than six months to run. It's a great opportunity. I can hardly throw it up.'

'I thought you'd take that line.'

'It's not a *line*. It's common sense.'

'And you mustn't let your wife and son get in the way of that common sense?'

'Couldn't you stick things out for another two or three months? After that it'll get cooler and –'

'You don't seem to be able to get it into your head that our son is *ill*.' She repeated it even more vehemently. '*Ill!* You're so besotted with your life here that that's of no concern to you.'

'Anson isn't in the least worried. He's told you that. Babies can get these things, then they get over them.'

'But he's been unwell for weeks! Or maybe you haven't noticed that?'

For a while we tussled, like two wrestlers growing simultaneously more and more aggressive and more and more tired.

Then, decisively, she ended it all. 'It's no use going on with this. Mark and I are going to leave just as soon as we can arrange it. I don't expect you to move out of here. You can stay on. I'll go on paying the rent and you can keep the Caddie. I'll even go on paying your Miss Morita. When your scholarship has run its course, we can then decide what to do next.'

In recollection, my emotions at that moment continue, even now, to puzzle and shock me. I was horrified; I was consumed with grief and guilt. But at the same time I also felt, as at the sudden easing of an intolerable toothache, a profound relief.

# (25)

Since Laura has to go out to do her twice-weekly stint of voluntary work at the local Oxfam, I have volunteered to do the day's shopping.

'Are you sure that you can manage on your own?'

'I must manage on my own. I must learn to manage.'

'But I could easily do the shopping on my way home.'

'When you're hungry and tired of dealing with all those balmy people in the shop? No. Certainly not. In any case I must get out. Particularly on a spring day as beautiful as this.'

In the food department of our local Marks & Spencer I walk slowly and deliberately down the aisles, basket in one hand. Regularly I turn my head from side to side, so as to avoid colliding with anyone or anything. At one moment I all but trip over a basket abandoned by someone under the frozen food cabinets. At another moment I narrowly avoid walking into a woman who, swinging her basket, has pranced round a corner.

It is as I emerge through the swing doors that, failing to make those regular turnings of my head, I walk into a burly, middle-aged man in trainers, and, hardly in keeping with them, a formal, shabby black overcoat reaching almost to his ankles.

In fury he turns on me, 'Can't you bloody well look where you're going? Wanker!'

For a moment I think that he is about to punch me. Then, ends of the unbuttoned overcoat flapping, he abruptly turns away.

'No, I can't look where I'm going. I'm half-blind.' I have to shout the last words since he is striding so quickly away from me.

He walks on a few steps. Then he sweeps round and hurries back. He raises an arm. I think, curiously without any feeling of alarm: Now he'll hit me. But instead he merely touches my shoulder. 'OK.' He repeats it. 'OK.' Then he strides off to be almost immediately lost in the crowd.

On the way home I puzzle over the dissyllable. Had that OK

been a statement ('Well, now you've learned your lesson not to mess with me') or an interrogation ('No hard feelings, right?')? The more I think about it, the more it seems to have been neither of those things. It is like some password that I have either never had revealed to me or else have forgotten.

As I trudge home, the straps of two heavily loaded canvas shopping bags biting into my palms, I have a feeling of unease. Suppose I again meet him some time, somewhere? Will he recognise me. If so, how will each of us react?

# (26)

The departure of the Swissair plane had been delayed. Laura, stretched out on a leather-covered sofa, and I, perched on the edge of a tubular steel chair, were smoking in a strangulated silence in the first-class lounge. There was not a single other passenger waiting with us.

Laura leaned forward and stubbed out her half-consumed cigarette in a vast, hideously ornate crystal ashtray. She swung her legs off the sofa and, hands dangling between them, she stared at me. I blew out one perfect ring of smoke and then another. It was a trick that always amused her, but now she had either been unaware of yet another repeat of my silly little performance or had decided to ignore it.

'I hope everything will be all right.'

'It can hardly be that without you.'

'Oh, you'll manage. Selfish people usually do – and you're no exception.'

'Why not try to be nice to me?'

'Well, how about this? I rang Mrs Kawasaki at the hospital and arranged with her that I'd pay the rent by banker's order. So you'll have no worry over that.'

'That's very kind of you. Thank you.'

'Her son is about to arrive. So it looks as if things must be bad. I'm sorry to miss him. I'd like to have seen what he's like.' Then she resumed briskly, 'I've paid Joy up to the end of the month. But I've told her that you may not need her every day – or so late in the evening – and that you'll let her know about that in due course.' She reached for her bag and pulled out an envelope. 'And here's some spending money. I know that you're used to your little extravagances and that that precious scholarship doesn't go all that far.'

I hesitated and then took the envelope and stuffed it into the breast pocket of my khaki safari shirt. 'You're being very generous. Thank you.' I felt humiliated and wondered if that was what she had intended. 'Ring me as soon as you get home.' I looked down at Mark asleep in his cot. 'Poor little chap. Twenty-two hours is a long time for him.'

'Well, at least we'll have plenty of room – and plenty of attention. It looks as if we're going to have first class to ourselves.'

At the barrier I moved forward, intending to kiss her goodbye. But she turned away, to say something to the stewardess beside her, who had volunteered to carry Mark aboard in his cot. Finally she swivelled round to raise a hand in brief farewell.

I felt both rage and grief as I watched the virtually empty plane gather speed down the runway. Then, though surrounded on all sides by hurrying people, I was suddenly overwhelmed with the sense of my total isolation. Tears began to force themselves up, like violent, agonising spurts of blood from some deep wound within me, to fill my eyes and trickle down my cheeks.

Without any of Laura's adroitness at handling the Cadillac, I had deliberately placed it at the far end of the car park, since it seemed that there it would be least likely to get hemmed in by other cars. But one inconsiderate driver had parked a van closely behind it and another a battered Wolseley saloon even more closely in front. Swearing under my breath ('Cunts! Fucking cunts! Oh, shit!'), I clumsily manoeuvred the Cadillac back and forth. Then I felt a violent jolt and heard the screech of the brakes that I had hurriedly applied. I jumped out, the engine still running. The bumper of the Wolseley had a dent in it. One of the headlights of the Cadillac had been knocked askew and been smashed. The broken glass crunched under my boots as I moved closer to inspect the damage. I knew, from past experience, that to replace the smashed headlight would cost a lot of money. Most likely the spare part would have to be cannibalised from a similar prehistoric animal consigned to the morgue of a junkyard.

I climbed back into the Cadillac and rested my forehead on the wheel. This time my tears were not silent. I bawled noisily while thumping the wheel with my open hand.

↶

Joy arrived not early enough to prepare breakfast for me but so late that I had all but finished what I had prepared for myself.

'Good morning.' She did not smile. Her face was so rigid

that it struck me, in my then paranoid state, as cruel and gloating. She made no apology for her lateness, but merely went on, 'I'd better start on some cleaning.' So fragile was my mood that I at once assumed that she was implying that I had made such a mess of things that she had better start at once on the task of cleaning up as much of it as she could.

Up in my eyrie, I tried to get on with the article that had already taken up so much of my time to so little effect. Then, giving up, I merely stared out of the circular window at the rooftops below me. A huge vulture, ominously low, was circling them, eventually to descend in leisurely, clumsy arcs and disappear from sight. It would be another scorcher, I realised. I'd be suffering the scorcher alone.

I heard heavy footsteps on the stairs. It could only be Joy. She was breathless when she entered. I often wanted to tell her that she ought to lose weight but always restrained myself. It was the sort of thing that Laura could have said without giving any offence. I couldn't.

'I'd like to show you something,' she announced between gasps, one hand to heaving bosom.

'Yes?'

'Perhaps you'd come with me.'

I followed her down the stairs. I could smell her sweat, like the odour of an overripe guava. The Japanese are so sensitive to the body odours of Westerners. How could that Japanese husband of hers have ever come to marry her, let alone copulate with her?

She preceded me not down the corridor that led to Laura's and my bedroom but along another, narrower one. This led first to a guest room and then to a room crammed with junk abandoned in it by previous tenants and perhaps, before that, by Mrs Kawasaki's son and his family. She jerked open the door, which emitted a snarl at the violence done to it, and announced, 'Look what's happened!' Beyond all the discarded objects – two massive cabin-trunks, a trestle sewing machine on a square table, some broken chairs, books saturated with dust, old, tattered curtains spilling from a cardboard box – there was a row of built-in cupboards. She approached one and pulled open its door. 'Look!' She sounded not regretful or vexed but triumphant.

The first thing that I saw was a glittering river of sequins, as the early morning sun slanted down through the usually bolted window, now wide open, on to one of Laura's evening dresses.

'She's left all these lovely frocks of hers. What made her do that?' She turned to me, like a prosecuting lawyer cornering the defendant.

'I suppose she was in such a hurry she forgot them.'

'What are we to do with them?'

'Well, she has so many clothes – not only here but at home – that she won't be in desperate need of them. So we'd better leave them until I can take them back with me.'

'But it'll ruin them to hang there in all this dust and dirt.' She looked around her with disgust. 'Oh, poor dear, she can't have been in her right mind, that's for sure. It's not like her to have been so forgetful. Is it?'

'No, it certainly isn't. But she had so much to do before her departure.'

She sighed. 'Well, I'll see to them. I don't want them to come to any harm.' Quite how she was going to 'see to them' she did not indicate.

I noticed a guitar propped in a corner and reached for it. I plucked one string, then another. The sounds had a plangent sadness for me at that moment. To whom could the instrument have belonged? And why had it been abandoned?

Shaking her head in what appeared to be disapproval, Joy walked over to the cupboard, its doors still open, put in a hand and raised the skirt not of the sequined frock but of another one, pale blue and made of the softest cashmere. Laura had worn it, only recently purchased, on the plane out, and then with her usual capriciousness had never worn it again. Joy raised the skirt and rubbed her cheek against it, like a cat voluptuously rubbing itself against its owner's leg. Her expression was remote and dreamy. I might not have been there. 'So soft. It might be silk.'

As we descended the stairs, she once more ahead of me, she turned her head to say over her shoulder, 'Oh, there's something else. I almost forgot. There's *this*. What d'you think we'd better do about it?'

'This' was a huge pink rabbit that, during the first two or three days of our stay in the house, Miss Morita had brought as a present for Mark. After Miss Morita's departure Laura had picked it up and stared into its glass eyes in hostile confrontation. Then she had thrown it across the room on to one of the two sofas. 'What a ridiculous present for a baby!'

'He may like it when he's a little older.'

She had crossed over to the sofa and had retrieved the rabbit. She had squeezed it. 'There's something hard inside here.' Her hand had explored further. 'I can feel some wire. It's unsafe.'

I had not seen the rabbit again. Now Joy was picking it off the lacquer chest where she must have left it before coming up to my study. 'I found it in the bottom of your bedroom wardrobe. Where madam kept her shoes.' Cradling the object like an unwanted illegitimate baby in her arms, she looked down at it. 'It's *ugly*, isn't it? I think that Japanese woman, that Miss Morita, brought it. People who don't have children never know what's suitable for them.' She turned to me. 'So what shall I do with it?'

'Oh, put it with those dresses.'

'You're not going to take it back to England with you?' She squinted angrily at me.

'I doubt it. Let's see in due course.'

It was, strangely, on my second night alone, not on the first, that I felt the full, shattering impact of Laura's and Mark's absence. Bicycling away soon after five, Joy had left me what she called 'some cold cuts'. Undressed, limp lettuce leaves and unpeeled and uncut beef tomatoes accompanied the slices of spam, chicken, and lamb that must have been in the refrigerator for a considerable time to be so dry and stringy. A half-empty jar of mayonnaise stood beside them. They were all far below her usual standards. So, too, was the pot of yoghurt with its synthetic mandarin flavour and cloying aftertaste of aspartamine. Was this her way of indicating that she really couldn't be bothered to take any of her usual pains with what I ate? I left most of the 'cold cuts' and half the yoghurt – partly because I would have had no appetite even for food far more acceptable and partly because I wanted to reciprocate her tongue-out gesture with one of my own.

During the summer the garden retained its heat long after the setting of the sun. But today a strong breeze had made it almost chilly. I walked over to the pond and stared into its dim depths. There was no sign of a carp. Were they all sleeping or had all of them died? Restlessly, I sat down on a wicker chair and then at once jumped up and walked over to the persimmon tree. The failing light had drained the still unripe globes of fruit of their usual brilliant colour. They hung there motionless like small, extinguished lanterns. All at once I could hear a bird singing from Mrs Kawasaki's garden next door. The racket (that was how I thought of it at that moment) eventually got so much on my nerves that I had just decided to return to the house when abruptly it stopped with an unseen susurration of foliage.

I felt an upsurge of longing for some company. But though I had made a number of Japanese friends, this was not a country in which, uninvited and unannounced, I could call on them in their homes. I might have called on Mrs Kawasaki on some pretext, but the house was dark and she was back in hospital. Rex was always glad to see me; but whenever we met, his strenuously over-friendly, slightly flirtatious manner seemed to be saying, 'Yes, I know you're not queer but I really rather fancy you.' The result was that, even when other people were present, I felt uncomfortable in his company. The Ansons lived far off and there were always those children, even late in the evening, with their boisterousness, cheekiness and even an occasional rudeness that their indulgent parents regarded as a joke. Katinka's establishment up the road? She would be too busy. And the Shotts would be too boring. If I were to arrive so late to see Miss Morita, her ancient, ailing mother would certainly be outraged.

At the far end of the garden I could see a wicker chair. Who had put it there? And when? I walked slowly towards it, brushed its seat with a hand and sat down on it. As I shifted to make myself more comfortable, it creaked ominously, as though about to disintegrate beneath me. Angrily I began to think of Laura. How unreasonable she had been, robbing me, with no warning, of both herself and Mark; and how cruel her contemptuous dismissal of the work that might bring me the university post that I so much craved. Her wealth enabled her, on the most fugitive of whims, to do precisely what she wanted at any moment that she wanted. Within twenty-four hours it was nothing to her to drive at once to a travel agent to buy two first-class tickets, to hand over to the husband that she was deserting an envelope stuffed with cash, and to undertake to continue to pay the rent for a house far too large and luxurious for him to live in by himself. She was spoiled, utterly spoiled. But spoiled people all too rarely spoiled others, as she spoiled not merely me but so many relatives, friends and fleeting acquaintances.

Then, as though an unseen hand had in a moment swivelled a searchlight from her on to me, it was I myself who became the target of the scorching flame of my hatred and contempt. For God's sake, she had been ill, and the ill were all too often not themselves. She had been in the throes of a mental disturbance, possibly caused by her totally unreasonable hatred of Japan, by her loss of that rich London life of friends, museums, concert-halls and theatres to be visited, or perhaps – yes, I had to face it – by an inability to continue to put up with my obsessive absorption in a subject that had absolutely no interest for her.

Now, leaning forward in the chair, I put my head in my hands and began to think, in no less desperate self-reproach, of Mark. My attitude towards him had all too often been that of a breeder to an exceptionally beautiful dog, horse or cat. There was pride, there was protectiveness towards a possession so valuable. But only intermittently present was the love that would have made me effortlessly and spontaneously sacrifice my own well-being to his. Distracted from my work by his squalling, I had more than once yelled at Laura, 'Can't you stop him making that bloody noise?' When he soiled his nappy in the car, I'd hold my nose in distaste, 'Oh, Christ! He's done it again.' If, taken up with some task for him, Laura left me waiting by the front door before we set off for some social engagement, I'd fume, 'Oh, come on! Joy's there. Let Joy see to whatever it is that he needs.'

Suddenly I was aroused from all this self-recrimination by a persistent whimpering sound. For a brief moment I thought, amazed: *But that's Mark!* Had the intensity of my sense of loss and guilt somehow, by some supernatural agency, brought him back to the house? I got to my feet and listened. The whimpering ceased and then started up again on an even more querulous and desperate note. I realised that it was coming from the corner where the wall separating the garden from the road joined a lower wall separating the house from Mrs Kawasaki's. Cautiously I approached. I heard a rustle from the high grass and, silent now, moving with extreme caution, a bedraggled creature slinked towards me almost on its belly. It halted and looked up at me from under a matted fringe of white hair. It let out a little, gasping whimper.

Other foreigners had told us how they had repeatedly come on kittens or puppies thrown over the walls of their gardens. The Japanese shrank from either themselves exterminating or paying for a vet to exterminate such unwanted creatures. But they thought nothing of dumping them on foreigners who, such was their sentimentality, at best might well take them in and care for them and at worst would deal promptly and efficiently with the whole murderous business of having them put down.

I stooped and clicked my fingers. With another whimper the puppy slinked nearer. I extended my hand to pat him. He halted, snarling and snapping at my fingers, without actually making contact with them. I said, in a cajoling voice, 'Come on! Come! Don't be frightened.'

Eventually I was able to pick him up and carry him into the kitchen. A mongrel, with legs far too short for his sturdy little frame and a comma-like dab of white over an eye, he was clearly thirsty and hungry – first drinking almost all the water from the bowl that I set down for him and then gobbling the wrinkled, half-eaten breast of chicken that, after another unpalatable dinner, I had thrown into the dustbin.

Satisfied, he began to explore the kitchen, whisking here and there until, with no prior warning, he all at once lifted a leg. 'No!' I shouted. '*No!*' But I was too late. The saffron jet began to flow, a widening stream, towards me from the stove at which he had aimed it. Oh, God! But curiously, although so fastidious about Mark's unexpected 'jobs', I was not in the least angered, but merely amused by this one. I picked up a cloth and went down on my haunches. 'You're very naughty, you know.' My tone was conversational. He approached, once again on his stomach, and then raised himself, frenziedly wagging his rat's tail.

⌐

Joy entered the sitting room, brush in one hand and dustpan in the other. 'There's one of those poos on the stairs,' she announced angrily, as though it were not the puppy but I who had committed the misdemeanour.

I looked up from the book that I was reading. 'Oh, dear, I'm sorry. Don't you worry. I'll clear it up later.'

'He's going to stink this house out. I keep finding them. If I'm not careful, I step in them. Hasn't he been house-trained?'

'It seems not. I'll have to start teaching him.'

'He's hardly a puppy now. That'll make it quite a task.'

'Leave it. I'll see to it.'

She made for the door and turned, 'You won't use any of my washing-up cloths, will you?'

'Of course not! Don't be silly.'

I'll leave some rags for you – out on the kitchen table.'

The 'rags' were strips from a pair of my pyjamas. The pyjamas were certainly ragged but I had not thrown them away, merely left them in the laundry basket for her to wash.

Later, as she served me my solitary lunch, she said, 'Well, I suppose he's a nice companion for you – the mistress and the little one being gone. But I was never a dog person, more a cat one. In any case' – she shrugged a shoulder – 'he's an awfully ugly little chap. Isn't he?'

From then on she never did anything for Bruin – as I had come to call him. She totally ignored him. For me, however, he was an inseparable and spoiled companion, who snored at the end of my bed, padded after me out into the garden, whimpered if I did not let him follow me into the lavatory, and jumped into the car as soon as I opened the door. Amazingly my efforts at house-training were successful in a matter of days.

⌐

Although I was still paying her what Laura and I had paid her, Joy arrived later and later and left earlier and earlier. 'I had something to do before coming over,' she would give as her perfunctory excuse for the lateness. For the earliness of her departure, she would merely say, offhand, that she had had something or someone (never named) to 'see to'.

When, at the end of the week, I handed her wages to her in an envelope, she shocked me by immediately opening it, taking

out the notes and beginning – ostentatiously it seemed to me –
to count them.

'All present and correct I hope.' My tone was sarcastic.

She put the envelope, the notes now restored to it, into the
pocket of her flowered apron. 'Thank you.' She patted the
pocket, as though to assure herself that the notes were still
there. 'Now I have something to say that you may find hurtful
and inconvenient. Or not, as the case may be,' she added with a
grim smile.

'And what might that be?' But already I had guessed.

'I'd like to give my notice.'

'Oh, dear!'

'The truth is that I like to look after a family. Not just one
person, as now. Somehow with one person I lose heart. It
doesn't put me on my mettle.'

I restrained myself from saying that, since Laura's departure,
she had been so far off her mettle that the food and her cleaning had both been appalling. Instead I asked, 'Have you got
another job in mind?'

'Well, actually, yes. With the German consul and his wife.
You know them, I expect.'

'I've never met them.'

'They're a very *good* pair. Informal, friendly. But the real
advantage for me is the children – five of them, all young.
That's very much my cup of tea.'

'Well, I can't compete there.'

'Would it be all right then if we made this my last week?'

'That does seem rather short notice, Joy.'

'Yes, I'm sorry. They want me as soon as possible, you see.
The Japanese woman they have is heavily pregnant. And she's
not up to much at the best of times.'

'Well, you must go when it's best for you.'

I felt magnanimous; and, although I had always disliked Joy,
I also felt, to my surprise, jealous. One never likes to be brushed
aside for someone else, however unappealing the brusher.

'I'm afraid I've still not been able to find the time to do the
oven.' She laughed. 'I hope there are not too many cockroaches
in it. I'll try to get it done before my departure.'

⌒

Miss Morita squealed in delight when she saw my new

acquisition. Hands on knees, she stooped and gazed down at him. Wagging his tail and head cocked, he returned the gaze. 'You are beautiful,' she told him – a conclusion with which, despite my love for him, I could not agree. She turned to me, 'What is his name?'

'Bruin.'

'Bruin? That's strange name. Why do you give him such name?'

'Well, it's not really just Bruin, it's Sir Bruin. Sir Bruin was a bear in a medieval epic *Reynard the Fox*. Do you know about *Reynard the Fox*?'

She shook her head. 'This is very strange. I cannot understand. Forgive me.'

'Well, don't you think he looks like a bear?'

'*Him*?'

'I think he does. A baby bear. It's something about those eyes – and the snout.' She was still uncomprehending. 'Oh, well, it was only an idea I had.'

'I will call him maybe Puppy-chan. That means, as you say in English, Master Puppy.' Again she stooped. 'Good morning, Puppy-chan. How are you this morning?'

Bruin growled for a second and then wagged his tail.

Usually when Miss Morita arrived each morning in my study I used to experience a vague exasperation. She was remarkably efficient in looking out sources for me and, although her translations were rarely elegant, they were always accurate and quick. But somehow both her appearance and her manner either depressed me or got on my nerves. This morning, however, after a solitary night and a solitary breakfast – Joy had still not arrived on what was to be her last but one day – I was delighted to have her with me. Seeming to sense this delight, she was far more skittish and flirtatious than usual. At one moment, when I mistook one Japanese word for another, she chided me, 'Oh, you silly boy!' At another she suddenly remarked gleefully, staring down at my legs, 'Oh, you are wearing different socks! Look!' She pointed. 'One light brown, other dark brown.' At that she lowered her head, covered her mouth with a hand and began to giggle uncontrollably.

'So I am!'

'I think maybe you need someone to look after you.'

This prompted me to tell her of Joy's imminent and sudden departure. When I had finished, she shook her head in anger. 'I think this not good. You pay her too much and now she behaves with no consideration.' How did she know how much we had been paying her? Laura could not possibly have told her. Perhaps she had told Mrs Kawasaki, who had then told Miss Morita. 'I never like that person. But I did not wish to tell. She is English and so maybe you become upset by my criticism.'

When she was leaving, she put a hand to the brim of her straw hat and looked out at me from under it: 'If you require me for anything, please, please let me know. I am very happy to help. Shopping. Looking after Puppy-chan. With Hoover. I am not a good cook but I can cook a little, Japanese style. Please telephone if you need me. Any time. I am happy.' She gave her little bow. 'So I say *sayonara*. Do not be too sad. So much in this world is good and beautiful. So much.'

# (27)

I am walking, at my usually slow pace, stick in hand, down Kensington High Street. It is foolish of me to do so, because today is a Saturday and on Saturdays the High Street is crowded with people, aimlessly drifting, suddenly zigzagging across my path or walking three or four abreast, in a way that makes me feel defenceless and disorientated.

Ahead of me I see an elderly man in dark glasses, old Army greatcoat, peaked cap and flowing red-and-white Arsenal scarf, dramatically swaying from side to side and bowing up and down as he plays the violin outside Boots. There is a pewter mug on the ground and beside it, as though accidentally dropped there, a piece of cardboard with 'Give generously' scrawled in untidy script and then below that, in capitals, 'BLIND!'. Usually I hurry past such people, making the excuse to myself that they are probably frauds and that it is far better to give to bona fide charities – as Laura and I do from time to time.

He is playing the Londonderry Air with an incompetence, all erratic intonation and clumsy portamenti, that at first grates on me. Then I halt, chilled and moved by the bleak pathos of the frail, solitary figure, the indifferent crowds and the plaintive tune. I often tell myself about my own condition: Well, it could be worse, much worse. Here is the confirmation of that. I put my hand in my coat pocket and find a pound coin. I stoop and drop it, with a clink, into the mug on the ground beside him. As I straighten, he croaks something. For a brief moment I hear, because of that previous experience of the man with the cropped hair, dirty trainers and long, black overcoat, 'OK'. Then I realise that what he has said is, 'Oh, thanks.' I look over my shoulder. I want to see him better with my little eye. How old is he? Is he wearing mittens? Yes, I think that he is but, peering through my little eye, I cannot be sure. I peer again. Then I hurry on – and in doing so walk straight into a woman.

'Sorry! Sorry!' The impact has been jarring. Then I hasten to explain. 'I have virtually no peripheral vision, I'm afraid. It's as though I were looking at you through a tunnel. It's an awful nuisance. Sorry,' I repeat. 'Are you all right?'

I now see that she is pulling behind her a little wicker trolley and that sitting upright in it is a small terrier – Lakeland, Border, Yorkshire? – its head tilted to one side and its ears pricked. The woman is middle-aged with carefully waved grey hair, grey eyes and a large mouth.

She does not answer my question. Instead she cries out, 'Oh, you poor dear! Then she adds, 'Would you like me to see you home?'

'Oh, no. No. Thank you. I can manage quite well. If I take my time.'

'I'd be happy to oblige. I've done everything I had to do – which was taking my little boy to the vet for an overdue injection.'

I walk on and then turn up Church Street for home, feeling suddenly happy. I even whistle for a moment, a few bars of *Sakura* that, so long forgotten, has suddenly and inexplicably come into my head. As I approach our gate, the man whom Laura and I call 'The Colonel' emerges, with his strutting walk, through the next-door one. He isn't really a retired colonel but a retired dealer in second-hand cars. But because of his exaggeratedly clipped, booming voice, his well-trimmed white moustache and his white hair decisively parted in the middle, he might easily be mistaken for one.

His wife is long dead and his numerous children have been scattered to the four corners of the world. As a result, starved of company and having far too little to do, he likes to waylay anyone, even a stranger, during the hours before he marches into the pub at the bottom of the road at exactly noon.

'Hello, old chap! How are you getting along then? Is the sight any better?'

I have already told him and innumerable other kind enquirers that it will never be better. But this time I cannot be bothered to tell him that yet again. Instead I say, 'Not very much, I'm afraid. I just live in hope.'

'Well, that's what most of us live in. I certainly do. Poor chap! It must be rather inconvenient for you.'

'Oh, I'm adapting.'

Then, because it is clear that he has nothing to do with the twenty or so minutes before twelve o'clock and because the incident with the woman has made me feel so unaccountably happy, I tell him about it. He listens attentively, stroking his moustache, his small, hooded eyes fixed on me. At the end, 'Good God!' he exclaims. 'D'you think she was a tart?'

I laugh. 'She was a decent, kind Kensington woman.'

'A lot of decent, kind Kensington women are tarts. That's how they can afford to be Kensington women.' Is he being serious or joking? I cannot be certain.

'I'm sure that this one was never a tart.'

'Well, bless my soul! Well, I daresay you know best.'

# (28)

It was barely ten o'clock. Sitting at my late breakfast, I heard the rubbish cart out in the street. It stopped, grunted and gasped to a halt, and then moved on. I turned my head and saw that the bin in the recess beside the refrigerator was overflowing with garbage. I should have put it out. But in my misery, everything seemed too much trouble to do at once and so was deferred from day to day. Soon, I thought, the kitchen would be infested not merely with cockroaches but with rats. I pushed my half-drunk cup of Nescafé away from me – Laura always insisted that we drink only 'real' coffee but I had not been able to find any at the ramshackle little store at the end of the road – and stretched out for the bottle of Gordon's gin, bought in Kobe from a lascar who had smuggled it, probably stolen, off the liner on which he worked. I did not bother to pour out a shot but raised the bottle to my lips and gulped. I bent down and looked at Bruin under the table at my feet. 'I'm in danger of becoming a drunk,' I told him. He returned my look and wagged his tail.

At that moment the bell rang and rang again. Who the hell could it be at such an hour? Might it be one of the dustmen, always so efficient, to ask what had happened to our bin? I was not expecting Miss Morita until the afternoon.

Bruin padded after me and began to bark as soon as I had opened the door.

Rex was standing there, in the kind of flowered summer shirt all too common today in hot weather but then rare except on a beach or in the countryside. His plump, exposed forearms were red from the sun, as was his forehead. Involuntarily I covered my mouth with my hand, in typically Japanese manner. Would he smell the gin on my breath?

'Am I disturbing you?'

'No come in, come in.'

'Is this a new acquisition?' He nervously looked down at

Bruin, who had abandoned his barking to snuffle away at what I hoped was not a flea.

'A foundling. Thrown over the wall.'

'Oh, we've had some of those. We take them straight to the vet for what's called mercy killing. But when one thinks of it, it's really merciless killing – having one of God's creatures put down. We always feel guilty and ashamed. But the truth is we're not dog people at all.'

In the sitting room he told me the object of his errand. The Council were sending dear old Eric Newton out on a tour – to lecture about modern English painting. He was rather past it now, poor old chap, but the CV was pretty impressive. Of course he and I were involved in different fields of art. But perhaps that was no bad thing – since each of us might have things of interest to impart to the other.

I already knew what was to follow. Like many lazy but successful people in positions of authority, Rex had a genius for delegating. He could not be bothered to escort this distinguished visitor from gallery to gallery, museum to museum, temple to temple and lecture to lecture. Who better to press-gang into doing that than myself?

'I'm afraid I know so little about art. Music is my thing really. If you could spare the time... All expenses paid of course.' He laughed. 'Generously.'

In other circumstances I might have said that I was sorry, I was too busy. But in my loneliness, I welcomed the suggestion. However old and out of date, Newton, former friend of Sickert and Augustus John and present friend of Duncan Grant and Graham Sutherland, would no doubt prove an interesting companion.

'Good show! I couldn't be more grateful.'

'Can I offer you anything? I've been remiss in not asking you earlier.'

He shook his head. 'Many thanks. I've so much to do this morning. Miss Iwai is off with some sort of tummy bug. I often wonder how real her illnesses are.' He got to his feet and peered out at the persimmon tree. 'I love that tree. It's so beautiful and yet it's totally without any pretension.' He turned: 'You must be missing Laura.'

I had told him nothing of her recent departure. But he was a man who not only knew everybody but also knew everything about them.

'Yes, a lot.'

'If I may ask – what made her go like that, so abruptly?'

'Well...' I didn't really want to pursue the conversation. 'Well... She couldn't stand the heat. It was making her feel ill. And Mark kept getting these fevers and upsets of one kind and another.'

'Will she back?'

'I hope so.' But I had no such hope.

'You must be missing her. She's a terrific character.' He lumbered to his feet and made for the door. Bruin padded after him. 'And I hear that Joy has left you, too?'

'Yes. I'm afraid so.'

'That German couple are incredible bores. But that won't trouble her, since she's such a bore herself, poor dear.'

'I don't really miss her company, I must confess. But I do miss her cooking and cleaning.'

'Yes, that corned beef hash! Isn't that her trump card? And of course those sausage rolls, of which she's always so proud! So – have you found a replacement?'

'Not yet. I haven't really looked for one.'

'I'll ask around, if you like.'

'That's very kind of you.'

'How about coming to a party I'm giving? I can see that you're a little down. The day after tomorrow, six-thirty. It's Masa's birthday.' Masa, I reminded myself, was Rex's diminutive, perky, restless, relentlessly amiable 'houseboy'. 'God knows how old he's going to be. It's now this, now that. He didn't go to Doshisha as soon as he left school. It was I who sent him there – when he was well into his twenties. His parents were too poor to do so. No presents, mind! You'll come, won't you?'

I hesitated for a moment. 'Thanks. I'd like that.'

'Your Miss Morita will be coming. She and Masa get on well. She uses our library a lot – not only when she's digging out information for you.'

As I closed the door on him, I wondered what sort of gossip he had heard about Miss Morita and me. We had, after all, been constantly together during the weeks of Laura's self-isolation.

⌒

I told Miss Morita that, if she wished, I would drive her to Rex's party. Then I wished that I had not done so. But for my invitation to her, I'd have made some late excuse and said that I could not come. I hated my isolation and yet the thought of company nauseated me. So far I had survived the day without a drop of booze. I kept telling myself that at the party I must not have more than one drink.

'Oh, you are so smart!' Miss Morita exclaimed when she saw me in the white linen suit, a present from Laura immediately before our departure for Japan, that I so rarely wore and in which I always felt a vague physical discomfort, as from something that did not quite fit, even though it had been impeccably tailored by Anderson and Sheppard.

'You also!' I was not flattering her. In her beige *crêpe de Chine* dress, with its pleated skirt, a dark-green silk scarf and high-heeled brown court shoes, she looked far more elegant than I had ever seen her. Her face was startling in the pallor of its make-up.

Giving a little bobbing curtsey, she looked up at me from under lowered lids. 'You are too kind to me.'

'Not at all. I mean it.'

'My mother says that heels of these shoes are too high.'

'Your mother is talking nonsense.'

'You must not say such things!' She raised a hand to her mouth – how I longed to pull it away! – and giggled behind it.

Masa opened the door of Rex's flat to us. To my astonishment he at once put hands on my shoulders and, even as involuntarily I began to back off, planted a kiss on each of my cheeks. In those days for a man publicly to kiss another was extremely rare in England. For him to perform that action in Japan was virtually unknown.

'Happy birthday!' I held out my clumsily wrapped present of a box of Scottish shortbread bought some weeks before by Laura in Kobe.

Oddly, his response was an enthusiastic repetition of my good wishes: 'Happy birthday!'

Miss Morita now held out what appeared to be a scroll, neatly wrapped in gold paper. 'Please.'

'In Japan we open presents later,' he explained to me. Then he turned to her: 'But I must know. What is it?'

'I have painted you a picture. Old style. Arashiyama. I am afraid I am not a good painter.'

'Beautiful!' Since he had not looked at the picture, this judgement was also odd. He placed our presents, still unopened, on top of a chest and announced, 'Now I introduce you.'

As at all Rex's parties, there was every variety of guest. In the course of the evening, I met two Australians, handsome, healthy and happy, who were on their honeymoon; a faded American widow with a narrow, pinched face, who at once revealed to me that she was about to enter a Buddhist nunnery; three obviously queer English tourists from Leeds, huddled together, heads close and far from delighted when Masa interrupted them to introduce me; various consular officials or foreign businessmen with their wives; and a number of Japanese professors without them. Whenever I became separated from Miss Morita, she all too soon rejoined me.

Two waiters, one white-haired and heavily lined and the other crew-cut and youthful, carried round trays of minuscule canapés. At one point, as I took one, Masa touched my shoulder as he passed: 'I make canapé. I hope OK?'

'They're terrific.' But already he had moved out of earshot.

Greedily I grabbed glass after glass of champagne and drained each in a few feverish gulps. Suddenly I noticed the look of alarm on Miss Morita's face as I stretched my hand out over her shoulder for yet another.

Rex came up to us. He had a glass of champagne in each hand. One tilted as he moved towards me and champagne splashed on my trouser leg. He made no apology, presumably unaware.

'Are you enjoying yourself?'

'Hugely.'

'I wanted to cheer you up. When I called the other day, you seemed to be so down.'

'I'm not down now. In fact I'm up. Very much up.'

Suddenly I realised that I was far up on the way to being drunk.

'Well, that's how we want it. Oh, by the way, you remember that I volunteered to look for someone to take the place of the joyless Joy? Well, I think that I've found the perfect person. I invited him to come this evening but he had to work late. He's a barman at the Miyako hotel – that's where I met him. But he isn't getting on well with the manager and wants to move on. Before the Miyako he was houseboy to a French diplomat in Tokyo. He strikes me as a good egg. Would you like to see him?'

'Why not?'

He put a hand on my shoulder, with a laugh. 'Don't look so apprehensive. He's not in the least queer – as far as I can gather. When I try to flirt with him at the bar, he usually moves off and starts to polish glasses. So how about it?'

'Fine. Thank you.'

'Then I'll give him your name and number. He speaks both French and English. Not at all badly. He graduated from Waseda – in English, I think.'

'It's odd that a Waseda graduate is a houseboy.'

He leaned forward and lowered his voice: 'I think the problem may be that his family came from Korea – brought here before the war. Even today Koreans are very much second-class citizens in Japan – like West Indians back home. As no doubt you know.' He looked over his shoulder. 'I must take these drinks to the Waterfords. They must be wondering what has happened to me. I do wish they would mix. They have such a look of bewildered superiority at all my parties.' Waterford was American Consul-General in Osaka.

Miss Morita appeared yet again. 'I think we must go.' It was not an interrogative. She was clearly worried that I might in some way make a fool or an exhibition of myself.

I produced the usual protest of drunks in such circumstances: 'But I'm just beginning to enjoy myself.'

She linked her arm in mine. 'Please. Come.'

⌒

It was only as I began to drive the car down the main street of the city that I finally realised how drunk I was. She put a hand on my arm. 'Take care!' Jumping the lights just as they had changed, I had all but collided with a van.

'Whoops! That was a close shave.'

'You must drive more slowly.'

'I'll try.'

The streetlights seemed unusually glaring and the wheel of the car unusually recalcitrant, despite the power steering.

'I'll drop you off at your house,' I said.

'No, no, thank you. No need. On such a beautiful evening I can walk. Not far.'

'Oh, I can't let you do that. You might get... way-way-way-laid.' I shook my head in exasperation as though that would somehow dislodge from my brain the word that I was stammering over.

'In any case I wish to pick up that article by Professor Matsumoto on Nagahide Choshu. You remember? You want me to translate it tomorrow.' She would rarely write out a translation for me, but instead, having gone through the text the previous evening, she would deliver it impromptu – frowning from time to time as she hesitated over something difficult and then looking up at me, relieved or even delighted, when she was able to produce its exact English equivalent. 'I must look over before I come to you. Professor Matsumoto is not so easy a writer. Good, interesting, but not easy.'

When we reached the house, I told her that, if she would like to wait in the car, I'd go and fetch the book. But she at once opened her door and began to get out. As she did so, I again noticed how, unlike most Japanese women of that period, she had remarkably long and well-shaped legs. 'I will come with you. I do not wish to make trouble.'

My attraction to her was like a sudden thirst, demanding at once to be slaked. I had a crazy desire to put my arms around her as she preceded me into the house and then to pull her round and hold her to me. I opened the door to the sitting room and switched on the light. Bruin, who had been asleep on an armchair, jumped off it, tail wagging, to greet us. I was acutely aware of a strong canine smell. He jumped up at Miss Morita, making her recoil with a little squeal. I felt a momentary shame that, always so tidy and clean when Joy was working for us, the room was now such a mess. The long, low lacquered table, between two sofas piled with newspapers and books, even had on it a mug with dregs of coffee in it and a plate encrusted with granules of dried scrambled egg.

I gave a mock Japanese bow and indicated, by mistake, the armchair so recently vacated by Bruin. She squinted at it, covered as it was with hairs, and then crossed to another one. 'I'll fetch you the article. It's not here, I think.' I turned over a pile of newspapers and periodicals on the sofa, causing some of them to glide to the floor. 'No. Not here. No.'

Miss Morita had jumped up and begun to pick up what I had dislodged. As she straightened she cried out in horror, 'No, no!' As though he had caught an infection of his master's lust, Bruin had embraced one of those long, shapely legs between his two short front ones and, tongue a crimson streamer, was jerking up and down. She thrust him away and gave an embarrassed giggle. 'He is a bad Puppy-chan to do such thing to a lady.'

'I'm tempted also to be bad.'

She ignored that, perhaps distracted by again having to thrust away the dog.

'If you don't mind my leaving you to Bruin's advances, I'll pop upstairs for that article.'

'No, no, I will go. I do not wish to make you trouble.'

'No trouble. None at all.' But the stairs winding up to my tower study seemed surprisingly troublesome as I negotiated them first up and then, even more difficult, down.

I handed the journal to her. She had already jumped to her feet on my re-entry.

'Now – how about a drink?'

She shook her head, with that giggle that previously had always caused me a vague exasperation but that now struck me as, yes, attractive, even sexy. 'No, no – no drink. We have had too much drink already.'

'Oh, come one! I'm going to have one.'

Even more decisively she again shook her head. 'Maybe coffee.'

'Oh, all right. If you insist. But I'm going to have another G and T.'

'G and T?'

'Gin and tonic.'

'Please. No. Not good idea.'

But I was already pouring the gin into a tumbler.

'Too much!' she cried out in alarm. Then she moved towards

FRANCIS KING

the door: 'I will make coffee. I will make two coffee. One for me, one for you.'

On an uncontrollable impulse, I went up behind her, put my arms around her, and held her close to me. Briefly she struggled, with a whimpering sound that, unnervingly, reminded me of Mark when he was angry or afraid. Then she swivelled round and returned my embrace, gripping my shoulders with a passion and strength that astonished me. I kissed her and she accepted that. But when, with my tongue, I tried to force open her mouth, she made a barrier of her lips. From behind that barrier emerged an odd 'Mm-mm-mm'.

I toppled her on to the sofa and put a hand over one of her breasts. She squirmed, kicking out with those legs that were for me her major attraction, but allowed the hand to remain where it was. Her head was now resting against the back of the sofa; her eyes were firmly shut. She might have been about to endure some unpleasant procedure in a dentist's chair, without an anaesthetic.

Again I pushed my tongue through the barrier of those unwelcoming lips. Again that strange 'Mm-mm-mm' emerged. My other hand tweaked at her skirt and then went under it. Simultaneously she opened her eyes wide in terror and floundered out of any contact with me.

'Oh, come on!'

For a while she stared ahead, expressionless, but frowning as though she were working out some difficult sum. Then, having reached a decision, she went down on her knees in front of me and with delicate slowness began to undo the buttons of my fly. I put my hand on the back of her neck as I felt her fingers at the base of my penis and her lips closing over it.

'Ah!' The sound erupted from me. But a little later, in bewilderment and consternation, I muttered, 'Sorry. This just isn't working. I don't know why.' Louder I repeated, 'This just isn't working. It must be all that drink.'

Abruptly she abandoned my flaccid cock and once again put her head back on the sofa, eyes tightly closed. She raised her hands slowly to cover her face. There was a little gasp-like sob, then another. I tried to put a comforting arm around her but she at once shifted sideways, hands still over face.

'I'm sorry. This has never happened before.' That was not

138

strictly accurate. To be truthful, I should have said, 'This has rarely happened before.'

She got to her feet. Except for damp cheeks, there was absolutely no indication of the previous outburst of emotion.

'I will go now.' She stooped and patted Bruin, who, head cocked, was looking up at her, no doubt in the hope of a walk even at this late hour. 'Goodbye, Puppy-chan.' She sniffed, pulled a handkerchief out of a sleeve of her dress, and put it to her nose. She turned to me and made that little movement, half bow and half curtsey, that has long since become one of the chief things that I associate with her. 'See you again,' she said. Then she exclaimed, 'I am forgetting! The article!' She hurried over to the low table between the two sofas and picked it up from where I had left it. 'When I get home, I will read. Don't worry. I will prepare it for tomorrow. No problem.'

I hurried after her to the front door. 'Let me drive you home.'

She shook her head violently. 'No! You are tired. You are also' – she gave her little giggle behind the copy of the article now raised to cover her mouth – 'maybe drunk, I think. You must be more careful. Not good.'

I watched her as she walked, head erect and high heels clicking decisively, to the gate in the high wall. She pulled it towards her and then walked out into the night.

⤺

I drank half a tumbler of neat gin, in a rapid sequence of gulps, and stumbled up to the bedroom, fell on to the bed, and almost at once was asleep. Two or three hours later I awoke. The light was on, Bruin was snoring beside me, there was a hammering in my head, and my mouth felt as though it were full of cinders. I staggered up and over to the window, its curtains left undrawn, and stared out into the empty street. I fumbled for the packet of Camels and the cigarette lighter in the usual drawer, lit one and drew heavily on it. My stomach lurched and, after another deep inhalation, I stubbed the cigarette out in the saucer of a half-empty cup of coffee that had remained on the dressing table for days. Clutching the banister, I went down the stairs and out into the garden. Bruin must have been behind me, but I became aware of him only when he settled himself, with a grunt, at my feet by the wicker chair.

I was in a turmoil of guilt and dread. What an idiot I had been! I needed Miss Morita for my work. That was why I had constantly defended her presence when Laura had attacked it: 'Don't you understand? I need her, I *need* her. Without her I can't manage.' But at the same time, after what had occurred, I could not face her, even if she came to the decision that she could face me. The night was cool but certainly not cold. Nonetheless I began to shiver uncontrollably. Bruin had by then wandered off. I could hear a rustle of undergrowth and then a snuffling sound. All at once I realised that a light in an upstairs bedroom of Mrs Kawasaki's house and another in the downstairs sitting room were still on. No doubt, anxious about his mother, Dr Kawasaki also could not sleep.

As dawn began to break and the garden was full of the chirping of birds, I got up from the chair. Not merely my hands and feet but also, oddly, my face were feeling cold and numb. Hugging myself, I stared into the pond. Far down in its murky depths I glimpsed a flash of gold. So I had been wrong when I had thought that all the carp had died! Once more I staggered into the house, leaving the French windows wide open for any opportunistic burglar, dragged myself up the stairs and fell once more across the bed.

⤺

At half-past seven, having been unable even to think of breakfast, I was up in my study. I picked up an American coffeetable book, lavishly illustrated, about *ukiyo-e*. Laura had seen it in a Kobe bookshop and, with her usual generosity, had at once bought it for me. I turned the pages slowly, looking at the prints. My hand trembled as I did so. I took little in.

Life in Japan began early. Only a few minutes after eight I heard a key turning in the front door and Bruin then yapping excitedly. 'Puppy-chan! Good morning Puppy-chan!' Now she was coming up the stairs. My head and heart both seemed to throb in time to that measured tread.

She came into the room. 'Good morning. It is not so hot today.' It was always 'It is not so hot today' or 'Today it is even more hot.' She was, as usual, wearing her white cotton gloves. Slowly and delicately she drew off one and then the other. She reached for the envelope containing the copy of the article, from the chair on which she had set it down with her handbag.

She pulled out the stapled sheets. 'This style is very difficult. But I think that I have it correct.' She sat down on the upright chair on the opposite side of my desk. 'Do I start?'

Mutely I nodded. Then, 'Please.'

# (29)

I am on one of my regular visits to the warfarin clinic. Laura wanted me to have my regular check-ups privately but Dr Szymanovski told me that, no, it would be just as efficient and far quicker to have them on the NHS. Usually the punctuality at the clinic is astonishing. The time indicated in my 'Anticoagulant Therapy Record' is always precise – 9.05 or 10.44 or 11.22 – and there is rarely a delay. In charge there is an attractive black woman, slim, swift and coolly decisive, who remembers the name of anyone who has been coming for any time. 'You're so efficient, you ought to run this whole hospital,' I once told her. She looked surprised, perhaps even displeased. Did she think that I was being ironic?

Today, for once, the clinic is running late. One of the two doctors in charge of the surgery, with his thick glasses and halo of white, disordered hair is new to me. He might, I suspect, be a locum. I'm sitting outside his door, which curiously, unlike his predecessor, he leaves open to reception, and so I can see and hear everything. He has none of the jolly briskness of the other doctors that I have encountered. The sad truth is that he is too considerate and kind to be efficient at his job. I can hear patients carrying on rambling conversations with him, relating the whole history of their strokes and heart-attacks or complaining of what they are convinced are side effects of warfarin. Just now an elderly woman is telling him of 'this awful itching, well, er, *behind* – it's driving me crazy' and asking if 'this medicine' is to blame. Head tilted sideways and towards her – might he be deaf? – he makes no effort to interrupt her.

It entertains me to listen to things of this kind, however bizarre and time-consuming, but the elderly, ascetic-looking man seated next to me, an elegant Malacca cane between his knees and his long hands resting, one over the other, on its silver handle, is fuming. 'Oh, get on, get on!' he mutters, as the woman now leans forward to confide, 'Of course it might have nothing to do with the warfarin. It might be caused by the

142

Normacol that Dr Burt – my GP – has advised me to take. Do you think that might be it?'

My elderly neighbour now turns to me. In what in my youth would have been called an 'Oxford' accent, he says, 'I always regard this place as an anteroom to hell.'

I merely smile and nod. I think about that. An anteroom to hell? I look around at all the elderly and ancient people, many in wheelchairs, with zimmers or with sticks, waiting their turn. No, not an anteroom to hell, at least I hope not. But certainly an anteroom to death.

# (30)

The first thing that I noticed about him was that he was carrying a large, battered suitcase, secured with a thick, hairy cord. So far from being an elegant object, it suggested abject penury. But his own person certainly did not suggest that. Despite the heat, admittedly now flagging, he was wearing a shiny grey suit, all three buttons of which were fastened, a white shirt with a wine-red silk tie, and well-polished, extremely narrow black shoes.

'Good morning, sir. I am Kanaseki. Hiro,' he added. With a small grimace, he edged away from Bruin, who was jumping up to greet him.

'Bruin! Stop that! Get down! *Down!*'

Bruin, as always when greeting or confronting a visitor, was slow to obey. I grabbed him and lifted him, wriggling, into my arms.

'He's quite harmless. He just gets over-excited.'

'It is new fashion in Japan to keep dogs in house.'

'Come in. Put that suitcase down there. Let's have a little talk.'

I gestured to him to enter the sitting room ahead of me; but, head lowered, he was determined not to do so. He even waited until I was seated before sitting down in the chair opposite to mine. His whole torso was unnaturally erect and he held his head no less unnaturally high. As he clasped his hands, I noticed how beautiful they were, with long fingers and nails buffed to a sheen. I also soon noticed how beautiful he was, despite the dark rings round his eyes, his extremely pale complexion and a general air of physical fragility.

I soon felt, as before with Joy, that the interviewee was really interviewing the interviewer. For each tentative question put by myself, there were at least two bold ones put by him. What had brought me to Japan? How long was I planning to stay? Was I living alone in the house? Would my wife be returning? His voice was low and slightly husky. From time to time he would

144

give a small, nervous cough, a hand raised to his mouth. I noticed the gold band on his wedding finger. He had no compunction in enquiring about my private life; but although I was curious to know if the band indicated that he was married, I did not put the question.

Would he like to see the rooms? The house was a large one and there were a number of them, I said. He could choose which suited him best. He appraised each in turn, uttering little. At one point, in a room that had its own washbasin, he went over and tried the taps. At another he merely stood at the window for a while, staring out across the garden as though deep in thought. Eventually, to my astonishment, he opted for what had always seemed to me the most unattractive of all the rooms on offer. Box-like and entered by a door from the kitchen, it had a small, high window overlooking the yard. There was little furniture in it and that of poor quality, and one of the soiled pale-green corduroy curtains was sagging from its rail.

'Are you sure this is the room you like best?'

He nodded. 'If I come, this room is good for me.'

'But to get to it you have to go through the kitchen.'

'No problem.' He gave a small, elusive, faintly ironic smile, with which I was later to become all too familiar. 'If I come, I will be often in kitchen.'

After our tour of inspection we returned to the sitting room. As before he waited for me to be seated before sitting down.

'You wish for reference?'

'Well, yes. I suppose so. That's the usual formality, isn't it?'

'I have letter from Monsieur Daladier – French consul in Tokyo, now in Africa. If you wish, I can also give telephone of manager of Miyako Hotel. But' – he made a little grimace – 'he and I not big friend. Monsieur Daladier very good man,' he added.

I began to read Daladier's letter, which was full of praise. I looked up from it. 'So you really think that you'd like to work for me?'

He considered for a moment and then nodded his head emphatically. 'Yes, yes!'

'Monsieur Daladier says you're a first-rate cook. Coming from a Frenchman, that's really something.'

'I like cooking very much. First I learned from Madame Daladier.'

There was no mention of a Madame Daladier in the letter. 'Well, that sounds excellent. Oh, one thing. Can you drive?'

'Drive?' He looked puzzled.

'I have a car. A very large Cadillac. Very difficult to manage in Kyoto, with so many narrow streets.'

'Sorry. I never learn.' His face lit up. 'But maybe you teach me?'

'Maybe.' But I was certainly not going to take on that chore. 'So when can you start?'

'Now?'

'You mean today?'

He nodded and shrugged his shoulders. 'Why not? I am free. I am ready.' He laughed. 'I have luggage. Tonight I cook your dinner.'

'Well, that's fine. Terrific.' But, having felt so enthusiastic, I now experienced a vague unease.

'We haven't discussed money yet.'

'What you wish.'

'Oh, no, we must fix that. Otherwise – who knows? – I might cheat you.' I mentioned a sum, generous for Japan at that period.

He nodded. 'I am happy for what you wish. But you must telephone Miyako Hotel manager to check me.'

'Yes, I'll do that.' In fact I never did. 'But first we'd better get you settled in.'

After he had followed me out into the hall and picked up his suitcase, there was a ring at the bell. I was about to go to the door but he forestalled me. He opened it to reveal an extremely tall, muscular middle-aged man in a beautifully cut, beige raw-silk suit and a wide-brimmed panama hat, with what looked more like a red-and-blue sash than a ribbon around it.

For three or four seconds the two Japanese stared at each other, the younger transfixed by the older. Then Hiro said, 'Excuse me. I go to my room.' Having hefted the giant suitcase, he left us.

The visitor smiled at me. 'You do not know me,' he said in a near-perfect American accent. 'I am Dr Kawasaki. My mother is your landlady.'

'Oh, yes! Do come in. I heard from Mrs Katinka – you know, of the boarding house – that you would shortly arrive. And now here you are! Please.' I indicated the sitting room.

He smiled, revealing regular, white teeth of a kind that, unless false, were then rare in Japan. 'Not now. Later I hope. I just wanted to introduce myself. I hope we'll see more of each other later. At present I'm jet-lagged. As you'll know, my mother is gravely – probably terminally – ill. So I felt that I must be here with her.'

'I wish I could do something for her.'

'Thank you. But now there's little to be done. We thought her indestructible. She was never ill. Until now, she had never been in a hospital except to visit me at my work. But sadly...'

'Is your family with you?'

'It was difficult to bring them.' Without elaborating, he put out a hand. 'I'm happy to have met you.' I took the hand. Its grip was professionally emphatic. 'We must soon meet again – either here or over at my place.'

After he had gone, I went into the kitchen and called through the door into the bedroom beyond it, 'Are you all right in there?'

'Yes, thank you.' Hiro appeared in the doorway, a coat hanger in a hand. 'Who is that gentleman?'

'Dr Kawasaki. He's the son of my landlady. He's just arrived from South America to be with her. She's very ill – maybe dying.'

He turned away. I hesitated, moved off and then halted. Over my shoulder I glanced into the room through the half-open door. Totally absorbed in the task, he had already begun to tweak at a jacket before slipping it over the coat hanger that he had first put down on the bed.

# (31)

At breakfast Laura has an infuriating way of spreading out the *Daily Telegraph* on the kitchen table, so that I have no space for my own *Independent* and little space for my plate or cup.

'Oh, I see that Rex Cauldwell has died! He was ninety-seven.'

She also has an infuriating way of reading out titbits of news that are of absolutely no interest whatever to me. But this one is.

'You remember him, don't you?'

'Of course I do. I've not yet succumbed to Alzheimer's. Or if I have, I've forgotten that I've done so.'

'One couldn't help liking him. Did you know that he was a CBE?'

'No. That figures. He progressed from one major post to another and ended up in Paris, the plum of them all. When I think back, the tolerance of the British Council in those far-off days astonishes me. Nowadays we keep hearing of this pink-ceiling thing in organisations like the BBC and the Foreign Office, but there was a time when practically every British Council representative was queer.'

'I never thought he'd get so far. Not I mean because of being queer. But he was always so *lazy*.'

'Yes, but clever with it. People were always saying admiringly that he could delegate – which merely meant that he had the gift of getting subordinates to do the things that he himself could not be bothered to do.'

'I wish we hadn't lost touch with him.'

I sighed. 'I wish that of a lot of people. Why did we let our lives become so narrow?'

'Because lives, like arteries, tend to narrow in old age. That's the way it is.'

# (32)

I was taking Bruin for a walk. That was the one thing that Hiro was always reluctant to do for me. Before going out for the day, I would say to him on leaving, 'You will give Bruin his usual walks, won't you?' He would rarely make any reply, merely nodding. When I returned, often exhausted from grubbing in libraries or attempting to communicate with some authority (almost always male in those far-off days) on Japanese art in my rudimentary Japanese and his equally rudimentary English, I'd go out into the garden to find dog 'poo' (as Joy would always call it) either littering the lawn or else, a favourite repository, piled in a small, malodorous mound under the persimmon tree.

Now, as always, Bruin was straining at his leash, panting and gagging, while I tugged to restrain him. For a creature so small he was amazingly strong.

Suddenly a male voice called out from behind me, 'Hi, there!' I at once recognised it as belonging to Erwin Shott. Eager to return to my work, I had no wish for the kind of lengthy, rambling conversation to which, after their initial taciturnity to us at Katinka's, he and his even more garrulous wife were now addicted whenever we met.

I turned. 'Hi!' I tried to look pleased.

'So that's the little fellow! We heard you'd got him. Hello, boy!' Shott stooped and held out a hand, the forefinger and middle finger orange with nicotine. Bruin responded by baring his needle-sharp teeth and yapping. Swiftly I jerked him away.

'You should get him a choke lead,' Mrs Shott volunteered.

'I don't want to run the risk of choking him to death.'

'That's the only way he'll learn,' Shott said firmly. 'With animals you must always make it clear who's the master.'

'That's something I've never been good at.'

'How's the new houseboy working out?' Mrs Shott asked.

I was surprised. I had not seen them since Hiro's arrival. Then I reminded myself that in that then tiny expatriate community everyone knew everything about everyone – even if, as was often the case, the parties had never met each other.

'Oh, he's terrific.'

'As good as Joy? It'd be hard to find anyone as good as Joy.'

'Oh, yes. Even better.'

'You must be kidding,' Shott said.

'No. He's like a robot programmed to anticipate all my needs and to do everything I want.'

'Sounds kind of creepy,' Mrs Shott exclaimed with a laugh.

'Oh, no, not at all.'

Later, going over the conversation in my mind, I thought of that word 'creepy'. Was he creepy? Well, perhaps yes, in as far as there is something creepy about perfection. As I turned my key in the door, he was somehow always present to take my briefcase and, if it was raining, also my umbrella, to watch me squat and take off my shoes, and then to select from a neatly ordered row the slippers that he had decided were mine and so never offered to anyone else. At exactly seven he would bring the usual bowl of ice into the sitting room and insist on pouring out for me the first of my many gins and tonics. He would then twitch a curtain straight or neatly fold a newspaper before giving his abrupt little bow, hands to knees, and leaving the room. He rarely spoke except to greet me or in answer to an enquiry of mine. From the start, he always addressed me as 'master' (in English). I remonstrated – better if he called me sensei, as so many Japanese did even though I was not a professor, or by my surname, or even by my Christian name. But he never complied, and eventually I gave up.

For all the hours that I might need him he rarely left the house, unless on a brief shopping expedition. He conducted what private life he had late in the evening, after I had gone up to bed. As I mounted the stairs, he would hurry out from his room through the kitchen and call up, 'Good night, master! Sleep well!' One of his long, delicate, perfectly manicured hands would be resting on the downstairs banister, one of mine on the banister high above him. He would peer up and I would peer down. Then I'd say, 'And you sleep well, too.' Later, with my then abnormally acute hearing, I'd catch the sound of the front door opening and shutting and the creaking of the gate into the street. Eventually I began actually to listen for them.

These nocturnal escapes from the life of solitary service that he had imposed on himself had begun to fascinate me.

His cooking was far superior to Joy's or even Laura's. With infinite care, even when I was eating alone, he would, like Joy before him, carry in the dishes and stoop for me to serve myself. 'Oh, just put them down,' I'd say, as Laura and I used to say to Joy; but he ignored my instruction. During the day he wore a summer kimono but for the evening he would put on either the shiny grey suit (I was never sure whether the material was silk or terylene) or a pair of dark-blue, immaculately ironed cotton trousers and a white cotton jacket. Often when I went to his room to ask him about something or for something, I would find him not there but in the intervening kitchen at the ironing board. In her haste to be done, Joy's ironing had been slapdash, so that on one occasion, when we were going to a party at the British Consulate in Kobe, Laura had insisted that she must re-iron the shirt that she had selected for me and so had made us late. Hiro's ironing was perfect.

When, one exceptionally stuffy evening, I entered the kitchen to ask for more ice, I was surprised to discover him at the ironing board not in his usual kimono but in only a jock strap. He showed no embarrassment, laying down the iron and then prompting me, 'Yes, master? You want something?'

'Oh, just some ice. I can get it.' With a mixture of curiosity and a surge of excitement, as though two leads had been applied to my heart to give it a series of increasingly violent shocks, I was taking in every detail of a body that I had never seen virtually naked before. The pale, narrow torso, totally hairless and the skin even smoother than Laura's, fascinated me.

'I will bring.' He turned to go to the refrigerator. It was then that I saw the shiny, diagonal bruise, like an oil slick, stretching from the top of his right shoulder almost down to his left hip. I was so shocked that I cried out, 'What on earth have you done to yourself?'

He turned, ice tray in hand. 'Sorry?'

'Your back!'

'Oh, I have fall. I get off streetcar and I slip. No problem.'

'But why didn't you tell me?'

He shook his head and gave me that small, elusive, faintly

ironic smile with which I had now become so familiar. 'It is not important. Now I will get lemon. Please. I come soon.'

Having set down the oval tray with the ice bucket and saucer of lemon slices, he said, 'Gin and tonic, master?'

'Yes, please.' As he raised the Gordon's bottle, I added, 'But be a little more generous this time.'

'Please?'

'Make it a big, big one. I mean more gin, not more tonic.'

Up to that moment he had never initiated a conversation with me. But now, as he handed me the glass, he looked at me for a moment with eyes pitch-black and oddly yearning and then said in a voice so quiet that I could barely catch it, 'Master, you drink too much. Always, drink, drink, drink. Not good.'

'No, not good. You're right.' I shrugged. 'But there it is.'

He was still staring at me. 'Why you drink so much? Why?'

Strangely, I did not tell him to mind his own business, but replied wearily, 'Because I'm unhappy.'

'Unhappy? Why unhappy?'

'Because I miss my beautiful wife and beautiful baby.'

'They do not come back?'

'I don't know.'

He tilted his head to one side and sighed. His curiosity seemed to have been satisfied.

'Call me if you want something, master.' He turned back at the door. 'Usually master has drink at seven. Now' – he looked at the Longines watch on a narrow gold bracelet on his wrist (how odd, I had thought when first seeing it, that he should have a watch so expensive) – 'it is not yet six.'

'Drink makes the time pass quicker.'

'You want time to pass quick?'

'Yes. The quicker the better.'

That was the first real conversation that we had ever had. In my loneliness and despair I now craved for others with him. When I initiated one, he would stand stiffly, listening but saying little. When I ventured to put a question about his own life, he would answer briefly and reluctantly. Sometimes he would merely dismiss the question – 'Not interesting' or 'I bore you.'

Dr Kawasaki was rarely at home. Early in the morning he

would set off in the large, modern Mercedes that he was either renting or had bought and would usually return at eight or nine. I assumed that he spent the whole day at the hospital with his mother. On the rare occasions when we ran into each other, he would say yet again that he hoped soon to ask me over. At last he did so, having first enquired if I played chess. In those days, having represented my Oxford college, I was proud of my skill. But he soon demonstrated, in humiliating fashion, that he was by far my superior. Our game over, he led me out into the garden, where we sat by a fountain, overgrown with weeds but still spouting, and drank white wine – an unusual drink at a period when it was whisky that was usually favoured by the Japanese well-to-do. So alert during our game, he now was clearly tired. He spoke of his wife and three children and then added that I'd be able to understand how he felt without them, since I too was now alone. At one point he asked what I had been doing during the war. I was a conscientious objector, I told him, working on a remote farm in Shropshire. He frowned at that and shook his head. Then he laughed, 'In this country they'd have shot you, not sent you to milk cows.'

'And you?'

'As a doctor I was doing a doctor's work.' Whatever that doctor's work was, he clearly did not wish to talk about it.

⌐⌐

A few days after my visit, I was sitting in my tower study. Miss Morita had just left, bearing away a number of things that she would be typing for me. Feeling unaccountably restless and dissatisfied, I lowered my book and went to the window. I could now hear two voices in conversation in Japanese below me. Dr Kawasaki and Hiro, the latter holding a trowel, were talking over the low wall between the two houses. Dr Kawasaki said something and Hiro then laughed loudly, throwing back his head, in a way that he had never laughed in my presence. They went on talking eagerly.

Two evenings later, a short time after midnight, Bruin started to scratch at the door and whimper – a sure sign to me that he wished to be taken out. I stumbled out of bed, pulled on my dressing gown, pushed my feet into my slippers and hurried downstairs. Arms akimbo, I stood motionless in the long, totally deserted lane and watched him go from tree to tree, cocking a leg. Finally he squatted by one and, a rapt expression on his face, began to strain and eventually defecated. Gladdened by this feat, he scampered off.

In the distance I heard a car approaching. It was a large black Mercedes. It stopped outside the Kawasaki house and two men got out. One was Dr Kawasaki and the other, to my amazement, Hiro. They talked for a little while in low voices and then separated. Dr Kawasaki walked deliberately, head bowed, to the one house. Hiro hurried to the other and skipped up the steps. Clearly neither of them had seen me.

I surprised myself by feeling not merely amazed and mystified but also jealous – or was it possessive? I lay on my back, sleepless, trying to work it out. A number of scenarios, each less plausible than the one that had preceded it, processed through my mind.

Then at last I fell asleep.

At breakfast the next morning, Hiro's air of chronic ill-health seemed to have intensified. The rings round his eyes were even darker, the greenish-white sheen of that miraculously smooth skin even more marked. As he set down the coffeepot, his nostrils dilated as he stifled one yawn and then another.

'I didn't know you knew Dr Kawasaki.'

Frozen, he stared at me with wide-open eyes. 'I meet him in Miyako bar before he go to South America. He is customer. In Japan barman must talk to customer. That is the way.'

'Oh, I see.'

'He is kind gentleman.'

'And last night he gave you a lift home?'

'How you know?'

'I had to take Bruin out. You didn't see me.'

'You saw us?'

'Yes. Soon after twelve.'

'I go to sake bar to meet friend. Kawasaki sensei is there. When he leave, he offer me lift. Very kind.'

Saying nothing more, I raised some toast to my mouth.

'He is famous doctor, I think?'

'So I'm told.'

'You wish something else, master?'

'No, nothing, thank you, Hiro.'

I had hoped that, with the passing of time, Hiro would get used to Bruin. But his distaste for the puppy seemed only to intensify. Could it be that he was jealous of my love for him. The idea was absurd, and yet... On one occasion, as he was carrying the cumbrous Hoover into the sitting room, Bruin, eager to enter, got under his feet. Violently, muttering something Japanese under his breath, he kicked out at the dog, which then retreated squealing. Clearly he had not heard me descending the stairs in my house slippers.

'Hiro!' I shouted his name. 'What are you doing? Don't ever, ever do that again.'

Hand on the Hoover, he turned. 'Always he get in way when I work. I cannot work when he come with me. Impossible.'

'That's no reason to kick him. You can always shut him up in another room or put him out in the garden.'

'He does not do what I tell. If I try to pick up, he run away.' He pulled a face and sighed. 'You do not understand, master.'

'Well, there's something I want you to understand. I will not have you kicking that dog.'

For a moment he looked sulky and rebellious. Then he smiled as he turned his head up towards me. 'OK, master. Hiro do what you order. Fine. No problem.' I could detect no irony. But I am always disturbed when people refer to themselves in the third person.

A few days later I returned tired and depressed to the house after a day in Nara. The two temples that I had wanted to visit had turned out to be closed for repair and an elderly professor appeared to have forgotten that he had an appointment with me. I rushed into the sitting room. I wanted a drink, a large one. I slithered and all but fell. I had walked into some loose, yellow-brown faeces by the drinks cabinet. In rage I rushed to the door, spreading the mess over the carpet, and shouted, 'Hiro! Hiro!' But, no doubt having heard me enter, he was already in the hall, rubbing one of his eyes with a knuckle. His usually immaculate hair was tousled. He had clearly been asleep.

'Look at these slippers! And look at that mess in there! I told you that you must take him out every three or four hours. I've trained him not to do that sort of thing. The poor creature must have been desperate.'

The more that I raged, the more contrite and submissive he became. 'Sorry, master, sorry, sorry! You tell me that if he disturb my work, I put him in sitting room and shut door. My mistake. I forget, I leave him there too long.' He rushed into the kitchen and returned with a cloth. 'Please. I will give you other slipper.' Suddenly he was kneeling at my feet. As I looked down at his bowed head while his hands eased off a slipper, I had an irresistible urge to kick out at him. The slipper off, he put it on the cloth, so that it should not soil the floor, and then to my amazement held my foot in both his hands. He bowed over it. 'Forgive me, master. Forgive me.'

'Oh, take the other slipper off and then get up.' The tone of my voice, harsh and implacable, surprised me. During the course of my life I have usually been the one who has been bullied, not the one who does the bullying.

He took off the other slipper. Then he rose off the floor. 'Wait, master, wait. I get you clean slippers.' He again knelt and eased first one of the clean slippers and then the other on to my feet. He looked up, still kneeling. 'You forgive Hiro, master?'

'Yes, of course. It's not all that important.'

Bruin, sitting on his haunches in a far corner of the hall, tongue lolling out, had watched the whole scene.

⌐⌐

After a visit to a remote temple, I had brought Miss Morita back to lunch. Lunch over, she was to help me with some work. Throughout the day she had been carefree and talkative. I had by now decided that, of all the Japanese that I had so far met, it was she, so intelligent, helpful and accommodating, whose company I most enjoyed. Surprisingly and fortunately she seemed totally to have erased from her mind that hideously awkward scene after Rex's party.

'What can I give you to drink?'

'Only water, please.'

'Water? For heavens sake...'

'Well, maybe juice.'

I shouted for Hiro, who rushed in with a bowl of nuts to go with our drinks. I began to pour out some gin for myself, as he hurried off to fetch the juice. He had totally ignored Miss

Morita's presence, as he now always did unless she addressed him. He set down a glass of orange juice on ice without looking at her and marched out of the room.

She came over to where I was pouring out some gin for myself.

Head on one side, she said, 'Please. No.'

I looked at her. Then I shook my head and continued to pour.

'You drink too much. It's not good.' By now I had heard her say that all too often.

'Well, that's how it is.'

With a resigned shrug she returned to her chair. 'Where is Puppy-chan? Usually he comes to say hello.'

'Oh, don't say that Hiro has shut him up somewhere.' I opened the sitting room door and began to shout, 'Bruin, Bruin!' When he did not appear, I began to shout for Hiro.

Where was the dog? Had he seen him? He shook his head, with an affronted, pouting expression. He had been very busy, ironing and polishing. Once he had let the dog out into the garden. No, he couldn't remember if he had called him back in. He had been very busy, he repeated. The French windows from the sitting room to the garden were now closed. Following the custom of many Japanese, I kept them like that during the heat of the day, opening them only when the temperature descended in the evening.

I went out in the garden, shouting the dog's name. Soon behind me I heard Miss Morita's piping 'Puppy-chan! Puppy-chan!' For some reason the sound infuriated me. I wanted to shout to her to shut up. Hiro, no doubt busy putting the last touches to one of his perfectly prepared and perfectly presented lunches, did not join us.

I looked through the kitchen door. 'Did you by any chance leave the front door open?'

He shook his head vigorously, continued for a few moments with shredding some lettuce leaves, and then looked up and said crossly, 'Maybe.'

'What do you mean, *maybe*?'

'Today I decide to sweep street.' At that time in Japan, instead of a street-sweeper, each household was responsible for the regular sweeping of the pavement and street area fronting the house. 'Maybe he run out. I do not know.'

'Oh, idiot!'

Miss Morita and I went out into the street. Again there was that shrill 'Puppy-chan! Puppy-chan!', now often followed by a 'Puppy-chan, where are you?' From time to time she even called, 'Where are you?' in Japanese.

Eventually we gave up.

'You must write notice. I will write notice in Japanese. Big, big. You must put outside house and other places.'

Gloomily I said, 'Perhaps someone saw him in the street and stole him. Or perhaps a car or lorry ran him over.'

'If he is run over, then surely we see the body.'

'Perhaps.'

We ate almost in silence. I ate hardly anything, but her appetite was, as always, sturdy. 'It's ghastly,' I said. I knew that it was ridiculous to be so much affected by the loss. But at that moment it was for me a catastrophe almost as great as Laura's departure with Mark.

Later, I realised that the adored dog had become my surrogate for the adored child.

A few days later I was alone in the dining room, while outside I could hear the melancholy sound of the rain remorselessly falling, as it had been doing for almost a week. All day I had felt so profoundly depressed that I had not gone out and had done little. For most of the time I had sat slumped in an armchair looking out through the French windows at the downpour. There was a murky, greyish-green iridescence to it.

Hiro stooped with a dish of bean sprouts for me to serve myself. I had guessed, from his elegance in his grey suit and silk shirt, that he was planning to go out once he had done with me. Suddenly I said in a voice of quiet fury, 'You've been using my Caron.' I put down the salad servers.

Still stooped over me, he turned his head to look at me: 'Sorry?'

'That scent – that Pour Un Homme – I keep it on the bathroom shelf. I can smell it.'

'I do not understand.'

'Of course you understand. Don't be so stupid! I keep it on

the bathroom shelf. Above the washbasin. Never use anything of mine again without asking my permission.'

He straightened. Suddenly I saw that his eyes were filling with tears. They remained on his lower lids like small beads of glass. 'Sorry, master, forgive me! I am not thinking. I smell perfume. Then – then I try. Only a little. Little.' He raised forefinger and thumb close together. 'Tonight I meet friend. I think that... Sorry, sorry. Hiro is very sorry. Never do again.'

I felt a terrible remorse. I had spoken to him so brutally over what was, after all, the most trivial of misdemeanours. I tried to explain: 'That scent – it's special for me. It means something for me. Do you understand?' I could see the look of puzzlement on his face. Of course he could not understand. And I could not tell him that I associated that particular scent, so insidiously potent, with Laura's and my lovemaking and so now, in her absence, with my memories of her.

When Hiro returned to remove my plate before bringing in the crème brûlée that he made to such perfection, I had a thousand-yen note ready for him on the table. 'This is for you. Enjoy your evening.' I patted the note. Wide-eyed, he stared down at it. I picked it up and held it out. 'Please.'

He hesitated and then took it, hurriedly stuffing it into the breast pocket of his jacket. He might have been concealing the evidence of a theft. Then he grabbed one of my hands, raised it to his lips and kissed it. 'Master is very kind.'

Embarrassed and amazed, I pulled the hand away. 'Have a good evening.'

# (33)

Two old friends are driving us back, far too late for me, from a dinner party in Stoke Newington. Ted always takes ingenious shortcuts, away from main roads and often down some street that is little more than a lane or through some mews with the cars parked on either side leaving little room for a passage. Cynthia is always telling him that his shortcuts are, in fact, longcuts.

The two women in the back are talking animatedly. Ted is too absorbed in finding his route and I am too tired to talk. I stare at the road glistening from a recent shower. Suddenly I think, with an extravagant leap of hope: Is this really happening? On such a journey it should be only the road, winding through the tunnel of my little eye, that I am seeing. But now I can see the pavements on either side and the people, often with open umbrellas, hurrying along them. Perhaps I have imagined it? I say nothing to the others. But I remain excitedly buoyed up by a secret hope.

Two days later I call to see Dr Ireland about the possible side effects of the statin that I must now take. Handsome, decisive and vivid, a lesbian I should guess, she is a new and revitalising acquisition to a previously tired practice. For some reason she has always seemed to be genuinely interested in the case of this ancient man who, like many other ancient men, has suffered a stroke. I tell her of my experience in the car.

She gives a sad, wry smile and shakes her head. 'I don't want to raise your hopes too far. That's a common phenomenon. In the dark the pupil widens and your range of vision is then temporarily extended. There is no neurological change – no change in your brain, which is where you have your lesion. You must ask Dr Szymanovski when next you see him. But that's my conclusion. I'm sorry. I wish I could be more encouraging.'

# (34)

It was my birthday. There had been no letter or card from Laura and all through the day I had waited, with mounting anxiety and despair, for a telephone call. In those days international telephone calls were cripplingly expensive. But surely to wish me happy birthday a woman as rich as Laura could make one?

Eventually it was I who called her.

'Happy birthday, darling!' she cried out. 'I was just about to ring you. Don't forget the time difference! I had to take Mark for some more tests. We've only just got back. Most of the time we were just waiting around. He hated that. You can imagine.'

'I thought you must have forgotten.'

'Don't be silly. I'd never forget. You got my card and the cheque, didn't you?'

'No. I'm afraid not. When did you send it?'

'Oh, more than ten days ago.'

'Are you sure?'

'Of course I'm sure. It's those wretched Japanese posts.' The posts in Japan at that period were as erratic as in England today. 'So many of my letters seem to get lost. I think that I'll have to register them.'

It was only much later, when, unable to sleep, I was sitting out in the garden in the dark, that I began to think about all those lost letters. Had she ever really sent them? Yes, she must have done, if she said so. She was someone who had an almost pathological hatred of lying. Had she been able to lie more freely, perhaps our relationship would have been more secure. Then another thought came to me: Might Hiro, picking up the letters when I was out of the house on one of my many expeditions, have destroyed them or hidden them?

Next morning, as I tried to eat my solitary breakfast, I surreptitiously glanced at his face each time that he appeared, in the absurd hope that somehow I'd find the answer to my question written there. But of course it wasn't. As always, the face that I was constantly bewildered and troubled to find so beautiful betrayed absolutely nothing.

~

'Have you given up working for Mrs Kawasaki?'

'Sorry?'

I repeated the question.

Although it was such a simple one, Miss Morita took a few seconds to answer. She put a hand to her chin, stared out of the window, and opened her mouth and then shut it. Finally she said in a stony voice, 'Yes. I have given up.'

'Why was that?'

Again she hesitated. 'Mrs Kawasaki is a good lady. Very kind. But Dr Kawasaki...' She pulled a face and gave a little shudder. 'He is bad man.'

'*Bad*?' I was astonished. 'Why is he bad? Has he been unpleasant to you?'

'You do not know?'

'Know what?'

'His story.'

'He's always struck me as intelligent and charming.'

Again she hesitated, staring out of the window.

'He was in prison. Six, seven years. Then he goes to Brazil. He cannot find work in Japan.'

My amazement intensified. 'But what did he do?'

At first reluctantly, with many hesitations, and then made voluble by her indignation, she told me the story. During the war years, Dr Kawasaki, a dermatologist of international reputation, had been researching the effect on the skin of poison gases that might possibly come to be used in the conflict. At the same time he had also pursued his own researches into possible cures for leprosy. For the tests carried out in his laboratory he had had the use of enemy prisoners of war. None of them had died as a result of his tests, but many of them had suffered horribly.

'I can't believe it. He seems to be such a civilised and humane man. How is it possible?'

'It was possible for many such people.'

~

By a coincidence I was walking down the lane the next day when Dr Kawasaki was getting into his car. I pretended not to see him but reluctantly halted when he called out my name and got out of the car to speak to me. 'I have that book for you – the one I promised. I've found it. It's not a good translation – made before the war, too literal, too ponderous – but it still gives some idea of Soseki's greatness. Wait a moment, I'll get it for you.'

I waited, although my first impulse was to hurry off. Amazingly agile for a man of his age, he took two jumps as he ascended the steps and another two when he came down them. He held out the volume with a smile. 'Tell me what you think of it.'

What I thought of it would hardly have been welcome to him. How was it possible that a man with such a history should have previously described to me a book as gentle, humane and compassionate as Soseki's *Kokoro* as the greatest of Japanese novels?

# (35)

Night after night, I try to recover those hours. Gradually in the murky bath of memory, sepia shadows of the photograph seem to emerge in disconnected patches. I see the museum, a spectacular building, all soaring glass and steel, at the end of a wide driveway flanked by cypresses. It is the creation of Mr Yamamoto, that billionaire collector of *ukiyo-e* whom I met so many years before. He financed the extravagant building and its park, and bequeathed to it his unrivalled collection of pornographic prints. It was he who, with all the generosity of a Getty, financed the purchase of all the other objects – works of art, photographs, films, condoms of every sort and period, instruments of gratification however crude or cruel – that are now stored in his Museum of Sex. It is extraordinary that a man seemingly so correct and austere should have decided to be remembered by such an institution.

I see him in his wheelchair. Since he was some years older than myself when first we met, he must now be in his nineties, even nearing a hundred. He is hunched, crooked hands clasped over a belly alarmingly large for someone otherwise so emaciated. His voice at first is faint and hoarse. But as his always silent attendant, a young man in a dark-blue uniform, followed by three of the obsequious curators, pushes him around from exhibit to exhibit, it grows stronger and stronger. He is particularly eager to tell me the story of one exhibit: a police photograph of a demure-looking little man of indeterminate age smiling at the unseen photographer. In a basement Tokyo room this machinist employee of a small shirt-making company had murdered a number of either professional or amateur prostitutes. He would carefully scalp them with an old-fashioned razor, and then himself wear their hair. That was all, Mr Yamamoto explained: the murderer did not rape the women. Briefly to wear their scalps in the privacy of his basement was all that he wanted.

I was amazed by the unemotional way in which he described

164

this and other horrendous aberrations to me. I was also amazed that Miss Morita's response was equally unemotional. At one point – yes, I remember that clearly now – the attendant removed from a display cabinet an eighteenth century dildo carved from wood cracked and blackened from age and handed it to the old man. For a while he stared down at it and then without a word, he passed it to Miss Morita. Impassively she looked at it. She handed it to me. Involuntarily, with a feeling of disgust, I thought of all those orifices of long dead people into which it must once have been inserted.

We are entering another room. There is a huge television screen at the other end of it. He points to a chair...

It is there that the negative in the murky bath of memory refuses to yield any more. There is a shiny black, irregularly shaped stain at its centre.

# (36)

Hiro handed me the chocolate cake that he had spent most of the morning baking and icing.

'Are you sure you wouldn't like to come with me?' I was on my way to a bring-and-buy sale at the Anglican Mission.

He shook his head. 'Too busy. Sorry.'

'It might be fun.' But of course it wouldn't be. I'd have liked myself to be 'too busy', but overburdened as I have always been, by a sense of duty, I felt that I must be there.

He shook his head again. 'Thank you.'

The whole small foreign community, most of them not Anglicans and some of them not Christians, seemed to have turned up. A surprising number of Japanese women, constantly smiling, were in charge of many of the stalls. One of them took the cake from me with delicate fingers and eased it out of the box on to a plate. She backed away from it in admiration. '*Beautiful!*' A woman beside her at the counter then cried out my name in seeming rapture, arms extended. 'Thank you, thank you!' How did she know my name? I had no recollection of that round, genial face, with its slightly protruding teeth and dark, somnolent eyes.

The Shotts approached. 'Hi!' he called out. He had a cigar in one hand and now raised it to inhale deeply and then to puff out the smoke into the still air.

'Good afternoon.' Mrs Shott was in a loose white blouse, worn outside an ample custard-coloured skirt with an irregular pattern of green and blue starfish on it. 'We gather that poor old Mrs Kawasaki is on the way out.'

'It looks like it, I'm afraid.'

'What news from back home?'

'Nothing special. Mark goes on having tests. Even the doctors at the School of Tropical Medicine are puzzled.'

'And the houseboy? How is that working out?'

'Oh, fine. You must come round soon to sample his cooking.'

166

At long last I somehow managed to get away on the pretext that I wanted to refill my empty glass with lemonade. From time to time other people, some vaguely known and some known not at all, chatted to me. They talked about the heat, the renewal of the security pact between the United States and Japan, the education of their children and the increasing difficulty, as Japan became more and more prosperous, of finding domestic servants.

'Ah, there you are – alone and palely loitering. I was wondering if you would turn out or not. Well done!' It was Rex, clutching a pottery bowl to his chest. 'Look at this! Talk about serendipity!' He held it out to me in both hands.

'I like it.'

'I should jolly well hope so. Do you know who this is by?'

'Not a clue. Has it got a mark?'

'Nope. But I have a hunch. I've become interested in modern Japanese pottery since I came to live here and I'm pretty certain this must be the work of Kawai Kanjiro. Heard of him?'

I nodded. I could hardly not have done.

'The best living Japanese potter – with the possible exception of Tomimoto. I've met the old fellow once or twice. Sweet old thing. Not that one ever gets much out of him.' He held out the bowl again. 'I'll show this to him. Get his confirmation. If it *is* his work then it must be worth a pretty sum. And I picked it up for two thousand – two quid. Think of that!'

'Wonderful.'

'Wonderful indeed. I've just got back from Tokyo. Strictly on business.' He winked at me. 'Life is fabulous there. It makes one realise how stuffy it is here. What are you going to do now? I've had enough of all this.'

'So have I.'

'Why don't we go somewhere for a drink and a chat?'

'Well, I . . .' I thought of Hiro, who would have my solitary, carefully prepared dinner ready for me at exactly eight. He hated the food to spoil in the oven. Then I told myself that this was ridiculous. I had come to think too much of his convenience and too little of my own.

'Oh, come on! I want to show you a little bar that's a favourite of mine. You need taking out for yourself. You need shaking up.'

I felt, though I did not say so, that at that moment I was so brittle that any shaking up might only cause every bone in my body to snap.

The Cadillac and his Standard Vanguard, provided by the British Council, were parked near to each other. 'I sent the driver home,' he explained, as he wrapped the bowl in a rug and placed it on the back seat, muttering, 'Mustn't break that,' more to himself than to me. 'The bar's not far from Hyakuman Ben. You know that, I imagine. I'll wait for you there and you can follow me for the rest of the journey.'

I trailed him down one dark alley and then another. Suddenly I realised that, though I had never before travelled along this route, we were not all that far from where I lived. The houses became smaller and the distances between them wider. The only light was what they and a large, low moon provided. We began to crunch over loose stones. There was a field with a narrow track running up one side. At its far end I could make out a low, thatched building with a scattering of cars around it and some bicycles leaning against it. There was a vivid electric sign of a rooster with, written above it in English, COCK BAR. For a brief moment I wondered if the letters TAIL had fallen off the COCK. Then I realised that the COCK and BAR were too near to each other for that to have happened.

'This building was once a temple. So at first it was called Temple Bar. Then a new owner took over.' Rex put a hand to the bead curtain and held it up for me to enter. The ceiling was high, with a single low-watt, unshaded bulb suspended from it to diffuse a murky light. There was one barman, an old man, in grotesque fancy-dress headwear that made it look, obviously in an allusion to the name of the establishment, as if a rooster were perching on his head. Six or seven people were seated at the bar on high stools, three leaning forward to talk to each other in low voices, the others silent. At the far end there were what I took to be three diminutive women in kimono.

The barman greeted Rex, who replied with a few words in Japanese – a language that, unusually for a foreigner, he had taken the trouble to learn.

'An off night, I'm afraid,' Rex said. Wriggling round on his stool, he pointed to a young man with the only attractive face to be seen. 'Be careful of that one. He's a little crook.'

'I'm unlikely to have any dealings with him.'

'Those three at the end are sister boys. Not my taste at all.'

'Sister boys?'

'Transvestites.'

'And I'm even less likely to have anything to do with them.'

He laughed. 'Yes, of course! I forgot. Is this the first time you've been to a place like this?'

'Yes, I'm afraid to say. Or rather – yes, I'm glad to say.'

'It isn't always so sad. A few nights ago I found Charles Laughton here. In the company of a Japanese dwarf. Perhaps he has a secret thing about them. No one seemed to recognise him. Except me. I went over and told him I thought *The Night of the Hunter* a cinematic masterpiece. He just replied, "Oh, yes," and turned his back on me.' He broke off to call to the barman to order some sake. 'You'd like it chilled, wouldn't you?'

I nodded. 'I hate these bar stools. They always seem even more uncomfortable than bar stools back home.'

'That's because Japanese bottoms are smaller and legs short-er... Tokyo was amazing. They cater for every conceivable taste. No feelings of guilt or shame. So sensible. Oh, I've just remembered to tell you. I met someone – a Frenchman – who knew your present houseboy. I can't remember quite how the subject came up but he had this weird story. Apparently the Frenchman, who's something unimportant at the Embassy, had a colleague there who was even less important. The colleague – let's call him Monsieur X – had recently got himself a wife. The wife had to go back to France because her mother – or father, or someone close – had died. Monsieur X then picked up your houseboy – Hiro, isn't it? – in some bar, the one, I think, in which I met his pal. Hiro eventually took up residence with Monsieur X. Then the day came when wifey was about to return. Monsieur X told Hiro that their affair must now come to an end, gave him some money and sent him packing. Monsieur X went out to the airport in his car and fetched his wife home. The couple approached the house. There, on the doorstep, was slumped what looked like a corpse. Guess who it was? Well, an ambulance was called and it took Hiro off to the hospital, where with the aid of a stomach pump and some other disagreeable things they somehow managed to save him from death. There had been a note, written in French, lying beside the body. Monsieur X had slipped it into his pocket but Madame X somehow later got her hands on it. It made the nature of the relationship absolutely clear to her. She left Monsieur X there and then, on the spot, and of course the scandal was soon all over the Embassy – and, in the end, all over every other embassy. The last news was that Monsieur X, now without his wife, was a vice consul in Chad or some equally insalubrious hole.'

I had been silent throughout the telling of the story. I had also been increasingly appalled.

'So that's the tale of your Hiro.'

I was silent for a moment. Then I ventured, 'I've often suspected that he might be queer. But all the time he's been with me, there's been no sign of it. Or of anything out of the ordinary.'

Even as I said that I thought of those evenings when, after I had retired to the bedroom, he would slip out on some surreptitious errand. I thought of that diagonal bruise on his back and the unconvincing reason he had given for it. I thought of the possessiveness that made him so offhand and sometimes even actually offensive to Miss Morita. And what about that sudden and strange disappearance of Bruin?

He shook a finger at me. 'Be careful! Be very careful.'

I hardly heard the warning. I was still thinking of his story. 'It's odd. Isn't it?' I said. 'To try to kill himself so publicly – to let himself be found not merely by Monsieur X but also by Madame X.' Instead of 'X' I all but said 'Daladier'. 'That suggests revenge to me. He *wanted* a scandal.'

'And got it! That's why I say – be careful, be very careful.'

I eased myself off my perch. 'I must be on my way.'

'Already? I'll hang on for a bit. One never knows one's luck. I'm sorry it was all so dreary tonight. Do you think you can find the route back?'

'Oh, yes. I'm not all that far from the house.'

Hiro had been waiting up for me. He came out from the kitchen to greet me as I entered the hall. 'What happen, master? Wait! Wait! I get slipper.'

'No, no. Don't bother!'

He looked shocked at a solecism so unacceptable in a

Japanese household. 'Please, master. You must wear slipper in house.'

'No!' I said it with so much force that briefly he cringed.

'I have dinner in oven. Maybe very dry now.'

'Sorry, I'm not hungry.'

'But I have beautiful trout!' He almost wailed it.

'Yes, and I'm not hungry. In fact, I'm going to bed.'

I did not turn on the light in the bedroom. I went to the window and stared out into the moonlit garden. Everything looked disturbingly weird, as though made of metal and glass. I thought: You must get rid of him. You must find some face-saving pretext, however implausible, to get rid of him. But then I realised that I did not want to get rid of him. I needed him in the house. More important, I wanted him in the house. Even now I am astonished by both the suddenness and the strength of an attachment of a kind that I had never known before and have never known since.

I began slowly to take off my clothes, dropping them on the floor. I knew that next morning he would pick them up, carry off those that needed washing and fold away those that didn't. I picked up the pyjamas, meticulously ironed, from the pillow of the turned-down bed. I looked down at the pyjamas; then I tossed them across the room on to an armchair. Naked, I clambered on the bed and stretched out on it. I was waiting. I hardly dared to think for what.

⟿

During those days an unaccountable restlessness would seize me, usually in the evening when I had had my dinner and was either preparing for bed or actually in it. By then Hiro would have usually vanished on one of his mysterious errands. I'd pace the bedroom or wander about the house. Sometimes I used to venture into his bedroom, now picking up some trivial object – his comb, a used handkerchief that he must have dropped by accident, a letter that, since it was written in Japanese, I had no way of reading, on one occasion a crumpled ball of tissue that I first unfolded and stared at and then slowly raised to my nostrils and sniffed – and now merely standing in the centre of the room and looking slowly around it as though in increasingly frantic search of something invisible to me. Sometimes I used to go out into the night, wandering haphazardly.

On one such night, taking now one turning and then another at random, I suddenly realised that there, ahead of me, was the low thatched building, once a temple, that housed the Cock Bar. I could just hear, coming from within, the hiss of an ancient recording of a nasal voice singing a jaunty, regretful ditty. I strained to make out what it was. Then I realised that the performer was Noel Coward, of all unlikely people, and that he was singing 'Don't Put Your Daughter on the Stage, Mrs Worthington,' of all unlikely numbers. I guessed that Rex must have presented the record.

Tentatively, as though some invisible hand were pushing me forward against my will, I approached the entrance and, without disturbing its glittering fall, peered through the bead curtain. Hiro was there, seated between Rex and, yes – I now shifted one strand of the curtain to one side to make sure – Dr Kawasaki. Hiro's head was turned to Dr Kawasaki and he was saying something. Leaning across the bar, head turned to them and grinning, Rex was listening intently.

I all but went in. Then I turned and began to walk away at a faster and faster pace. The air tasted odd in my mouth, bitter and sulphurous. Somehow I lost the way home and wandered for some time. Then I came on the noodle man and he directed me. I noticed for the first time, as he pointed to the street that I should take, that the middle finger of his left hand was merely a stump. How had I failed to notice that before? My eyes often played that kind of trick on me, even long before my stroke. I saw only what I wanted to see or expected to see.

# (37)

We are out on the lawn of the large, untidily sprawling house, at a tea party to celebrate my brother's eighty-fifth birthday. His wife is determined to treat me as an invalid. 'Is that table all right for you?' 'Are you comfortable in that chair?' 'Does the sun bother you?' 'Would you like me to bring you another scone?' The children, of which there are five, all successful in their different professions, and their spouses are talking simultaneously and rarely listening. The grandchildren are splashing about in the shallow pool. Laura reaches out from her chair and puts her hand over mine. 'All right?'

'Fine.'

'You're very silent.'

The truth is that I'm not fine. I have a terrible headache. Then suddenly I see sparks drifting up and away, as though from a bonfire in a high wind, imposed on my view of the children splashing in the water. An invisible cord tightens around my temples. Some of the sparks are now cascading downwards. I grip the arms of the chair. Then I stagger to my feet.

'Where are you going?' Laura asks, clearly alarmed. I wonder if I look as ill as I feel.

'Back in a moment. Loo.'

I think: I'm having another stroke. I'm dying. Strangely I feel no terror, not even alarm or surprise.

In the shadowy drawing room I sink into an over-upholstered armchair, my head back. I close my eyes but I go on seeing shower after shower and fountain after fountain of stars, stretching on and on into infinity.

My brother approaches. 'Are you all right, old chap?'

'I think so. I'm not sure. I feel so odd. And cold.'

'Perhaps I'd better call an ambulance.'

'No, wait. Wait. Let's see.'

He hesitates, wondering whether to leave me or not.

Then the stars vanish as suddenly as they appeared. I stagger

out of the chair and almost topple back into it, as my brother
seizes my arm. 'Steady, old boy!' He is still a handsome man,
despite the nose broken when playing rugby for England. 'Are
you sure you don't want me to ring for an ambulance?'

'Absolutely.'

In the car on the way home, I say, puzzled and wondering, to
Laura, 'It's odd. I thought for a moment that I'd had it. I was
either going to go completely blind or I was going to kick the
bucket. But I really do think my sight has improved.'

'Oh, if only!'

I can see that she doesn't believe me. But yes, yes, the little
eye has become a bigger eye. The tunnel is expanding slowly,
slowly, like the shutter of a camera being constantly adjusted,
bit by bit, to a different diameter.

# (38)

The telephone rang while I was having supper. It was Laura. As when her beloved grandmother, source of all her wealth, had died of a sudden heart attack, the voice was clear and firm. Whereas I always go to pieces in a crisis or disaster, she acquires an astonishing calmness and strength.

They – for her the doctors at Great Ormond Street, at the Hospital for Tropical Medicine or Harley Street were always 'they' – had now confirmed that Mark had contracted amoebic dysentery. But there was one thing that continued to puzzle them. Something was also amiss with his kidneys. He had some of the typical symptoms of nephritic syndrome – not usually life-threatening but often capable of leaving a legacy of chronic pyelonephritis (she stammered repeatedly over that word) in adulthood. But they were now investigating whether he might not be in the first stages of Wilm's tumour – a disease of which I had never heard. 'It's very worrying. The uncertainty is terrible. He's so incredibly brave, poor little chap. But somehow that only makes the whole thing worse.'

'I think I'd better get back as soon as possible.'

There was one of those silences when one thinks that the line must have gone dead.

I repeated, more loudly, 'I think I'd better get back as soon as possible.'

'Oh, I don't know what to say.' The previously strong voice sagged forlornly. 'I do miss you. I miss you so much.'

It was the first time that she had said that since her departure. I had said it – and written it – so often to her.

'Really?'

'Yes, really.'

After the end of the conversation I returned to the dining room, sat down and picked up my knife and fork. But I could not finish the veal escalope half-eaten on the plate. I felt vaguely sick and dizzy. Outside the open window a bird was making a clattering noise, three notes constantly repeated. I winced. Ever since her departure with Mark, I had been first exasperated and now haunted by the discordant racket of birds.

Eventually Hiro entered.

'Excuse me. I thought maybe you finish.'

'I can't eat any more. Sorry.' I put down knife and fork on the plate and then nudged them so that they lay symmetrically side by side. It might have been Miss Morita who had performed that fussy act, so unlike my usual behaviour. I cleared my throat, which seemed suddenly to choke with phlegm. 'Sorry.'

With pitying eyes he stared at me. They narrowed. 'There is a problem?'

'Yes. My son. My baby. I think – I'm afraid – perhaps he's dying. No one knows what's really wrong with him.' I put a hand up to my mouth. I thought that I was going to vomit but instead sobs began to jerk out of me.

He went behind me. He put his arms around my shoulders. He lowered his head and placed a smooth cheek against my rough, tear-spattered one. It was weird. That was how my brother had comforted me when, a small child three years younger than he was, I was particularly distressed or disturbed.

'Please,' I heard. 'Please.' Then firmly, 'No. No, master. No. Please stop.'

Like Englishmen of my generation, Japanese men of that period were expected never to weep. I drew a handkerchief out of my trouser pocket and put it to my eyes and then to my mouth. Hiro released me and picked up my plate. Plate in hand, he looked down at me. He gave a little nod – perhaps of congratulation that at last I'd controlled myself. 'You wish pudding? Apple turnover.'

I shook my head. 'I think that I may have to leave Japan. Soon. After a few days. I miss them so much. I want to be with them. What am I to do?'

He did not answer. I might not have spoken. Head and torso stiff, plate in hand, he walked to the door.

⌒

That night I swallowed three sleeping pills. I longed to glide into oblivion and to be free of my torment. After I have taken even one sleeping pill, my sleep is usually without dreams. But on this occasion it was seething with them. Other people's dreams, when recounted to me, amaze me by how sequential and coherent they are. Mine are always a maelstrom of fleeting images; all that is consistent in them is one dominant emotion. On that night, as I flung myself feverishly from one side of the bed to another, that dominant emotion was terror.

Even today I remember one moment when, in a sinisterly crepuscular light, I approached the pram at the far end of the garden under the persimmon tree. I stooped to look at Mark. His face was covered with a blanket. I tweaked it aside and there before me was lying not Mark but Bruin. His throat had been cut; there was a dark stain of blood on the pillow; his eyes were merely black holes.

I remember another moment, when, in the crowded concourse of an unrecognisable station, I was frantically searching, from platform to platform, for a train due at any moment to depart. Laura and Mark were on it. If I did not find the train, they would be lost forever. As I ran, I tripped over an abandoned suitcase that, with my tunnel vision, I had failed to see, and crashed to the ground. A horde of scurrying passengers paid me no attention.

I was woken from this phantasmagorical sleep by the creak of the bedroom door. The dawn, early at that time of year, was breaking. The light that filled the room seemed to be mistily opalescent. Out of it emerged a figure in the sequined dress that had hung, unworn, for so many weeks in the wardrobe in the little room at the end of the narrow corridor. I peered. It was Hiro, his face heavily made up like the faces of the 'sister boys' that Rex had pointed out to me in the Cock Bar. He was wearing a wig of long, thick, straight, blonde hair, similar to Laura's, and his eyes, perhaps because of the mascara caking the lashes, looked huge. He neared the bed. He looked down at me. Then he lifted the skirt of the dress and pulled it off over his head with a single gesture so decisive that I heard fabric tearing. Underneath he was naked. He stooped and with one hand daintily removed first one high-heeled shoe and then the other. He had never before worn shoes in the house or, if he could help it, had allowed me to do so.

He sat down on the edge of the wide bed, next to me. Then he rolled over, so that our bodies touched. Suddenly I smelled that unmistakeable odour, cloying and insinuating, associated with my lovemaking with Laura. He must have drenched himself in the Caron Pour Un Homme.

The whole scene was an even more terrifying culmination of the dreams that had filled the hours before it. With a violence that still astonishes me, I shoved him away from me, so that he crashed to the floor. He let out a sharp yelp and began to moan, head turned away and palms of hands rapping on the bare floor. I made out a muffled 'Please.'

I jumped off the bed. 'Get out! *Out!*'

I began to kick out at him with mounting frenzy, totally unconscious of any damage to my bare foot. He did not move. Except that I could hear his gasped 'Yes, yes, *yes!*' he might have been unconscious.

Then, suddenly, his whole body was convulsed as though in a fit. After it, he lay curled up motionless in a foetal position, his hand over his face. No longer frenziedly kicking, I stared down at him. I was simultaneously overwhelmed with horror and with the outrageous desire to possess and so destroy the naked body sprawled totally at my mercy on the floor before me.

Then I did something that I had never done or wanted to do before, and that I have never done or wanted to do since. I threw myself upon him. I all but throttled him as, an arm locked round his throat, I plunged into him as though to tear him into two. I began to thrust in and out with a mixture of rage, despair and passion. All the time I again heard his panting 'Yes, yes. *Yes!*'

Later, brooding on that act of frenzied brutality, I remembered an incident from a trip that an undergraduate friend and I made to Mount Athos soon after the war. We had hired, for a sum amazingly small by present-day standards, a donkey and its owner to transport our luggage. As we trudged behind animal and elderly man up and up a rock-strewn ravine, the already exhausted creature slipped and fell over. With rolling eyes it remained there, half on top of one of our bags, while the other bag bumped for some distance down the precipitous slope beside us. The owner, previously so calm and sunny, tugged and tugged with increasing annoyance at the tether. Obstinately, the donkey refused to move. Suddenly, in a frenzy of rage, his face red and contorted, the owner began to kick viciously at the animal until my friend and I managed to pull him away. The same sort of demon had possessed me on that fatal morning, with a man and not an animal as the victim of my savagery.

Later, after that night of fitful nightmares when my sleep had been so light and constantly broken, I slept deeply. The whole incident seemed to have become no more than a part of that maelstrom of dreams that had previously swirled inside my brain. Even now, in recollection, I ask myself: 'Did that really happen? Might it not have been only another of those nightmares induced by my loneliness, my anxiety for Mark, and my longing for Laura?'

When I awoke the next morning it was past ten. Always, even on an English winter's morning, an early riser, I had never slept so late during the course of my whole stay in Japan. I all but fell back on the bed as I got out of it. The muscles of my neck and arms were aching, and somehow I had managed to graze an elbow. I stared down at a small bloodstain on the white rug by my feet. I bent down and touched it, touched it again. Already it was dry. Could the graze have been the source of the blood? But there was no sign of a scab. The blood must have come from elsewhere.

I went into the bathroom and began to splash cold water over my face. Then, suddenly, there floated up from my unconsciousness the memory of something that I had read when in my early teens. As a birthday – or it may have been a Christmas – present, an uncle of mine had given to me a sensational, best-selling anthology of newspaper articles entitled *Believe It or Not*, compiled by an American journalist called – if I remember correctly – Ripley. It included one story that haunted me at the time and still sometimes comes back to haunt me. At the age of sixteen a girl in a small mid-west town had to undergo an operation for a huge tumour of the womb. When the tumour was dissected, it was found to contain the remains of a tiny embryo, the patient's girl twin, fated never to be born. When I had made my demented assault on Hiro, it was as though my own dead twin, for so long calcified in my body, had suddenly come to life, to force himself out as an entity wholly separate from me, before expiring from the demonic violence of his action.

Now, chilled to the marrow despite the already soaring

temperature, I pulled on a kimono and, in bare feet, limped down the stairs. My right foot felt extremely tender, and I winced at each step. Then the cause of the pain came back to me, as I again recalled, with horror and self-loathing, that relentless kicking and what, even more terrifying, had followed it.

I had prepared what I was to say to him: *Please go. Now. I never want to see you again.* But when I glimpsed him down at the bottom of the stairs, gazing up at me, I somehow found myself incapable of producing the words.

'Good morning, master.' The tone was neutral and natural.

I hesitated. 'Good morning, Hiro.'

'I will make coffee. You want boiled egg?'

He was now giving me, without any evidence of embarrassment or guilt, that small, elusive, faintly ironic smile of his.

Amazingly it was a morning like any other morning.

No less amazingly, I left it like that.

# (39)

'It's miraculous.'

Dr Szymanovski smiled. 'Patients like you always use that word when they've confounded a prognosis. I prefer' – he paused and smiled again – 'atypical. Anyway I'm delighted. This is one of those rare occasions when I welcome such convincing proof that I am capable of error.'

He opened the drawer of his desk and took out a small, oval box. When he had eased off the lid and placed it between us on the desk, I read 'Gold Chocolate Dragées' and, above that in smaller letters 'Fortnum & Mason'. 'Please.' He held out the box. I took one of the golden eggs and crunched on its shell. He took one and did the same. Then he replaced the lid and put the box back into the drawer.

It was like a symbolic celebration of my emergence from the tunnel and sudden rebirth.

# (40)

I had read in the English-language *Mainichi Shimbun* that Laurance P. Roberts, whose *Dictionary of Japanese Artists* I constantly consulted at the British Council library, was on a visit to Tokyo. After a number of telephone calls – to the American Embassy, to the American Information Centre and, on five or six occasions, to the Imperial Hotel only to learn that he was out – I finally managed to arrange a meeting. I then booked myself for a couple nights into a far more modest hotel. I had decided that, once back in Kyoto, I'd set about preparing for my departure to England.

When I met the pixie-like American and his imposing giraffe of a wife, I was able, in my excitement, to forget both my constant anxiety over Mark and my self-disgust and self-loathing over that strange incident with Hiro. After an elegant and extremely expensive Japanese dinner for which Roberts, a rich man, had insisted on paying to the ill-concealed disapproval of his wife, I wandered back to my hotel through the pleasure district of Shinjuku. Suddenly two passing sister boys, disguised as geisha in elaborate kimono and jet-black wigs above simian faces plastered with wet-white, rushed up to hail me. 'Hi, stranger! Where you from?' one of them screamed. 'Where you from?' the other took up. This was followed by giggling from behind disconcertingly beefy hands.

I paused momentarily and almost spoke to them. Then, heart and head thumping, I hurried on without a word.

⌒

It was late in the evening of the following day when at last I reached home. The express trains that whisk travellers at miraculous speed from Tokyo to Kyoto then did not exist. I felt not merely exhausted from the interminable journey but also leaden with fear and depression. I turned the key in the front door, in the expectation that at the sound Hiro, his hearing always so sensitive, would at once emerge, as in the past, through the kitchen door. But as so often when I have just returned to an empty house, I already knew that there was no one in it.

Nonetheless I shouted, 'Hiro! Hiro!' Then, getting no answer, I entered his room. It was totally empty, its window, to my annoyance, left wide open. I strode across and shut it. I went to the rickety wardrobe and tugged at its door. Nothing. I went to the chest of drawers. Nothing there, either. I stared, hands on hips, down at the bed. The sheets, pillowcases and single blanket had been neatly folded and left at the bottom.

I returned to the kitchen. Everything was spotless. The pedal bin had been emptied and its interior scrubbed. The rubber gloves that he himself had bought and for which he had refused to allow me to reimburse him had gone from the peg on which he used to hang them. He must have taken them. But nothing else had gone.

I felt an unrelenting sadness, even despair. It was the same emotion that I had felt in the immediate aftermath of Laura's and Mark's departure. My mood darkened yet further when I entered the bathroom. I had been complaining that the floor-to-ceiling white tiles were blotched with grime. Now clearly he had scrubbed them. When he had first arrived, I had indicated to him that the small cupboard and the shelf above the washbasin were exclusively mine. Another small cupboard, next to the combined bath and shower, was for him. The mirror above this second cupboard gave me back my pale, stricken face. I tugged at the door and peered inside. Empty too. I thought: You might never have been here. I thought: Were you just a figment of my deranged mind?

I was hungry. I was desperate to eat. I wanted some ice for the drink that might dull my sense of desertion. I went into the kitchen and took out two eggs from the ancient refrigerator. Then I looked around to locate a frying pan. But I consumed only a few mouthfuls of the omelette that I eventually made.

Later I rang Rex. He condoled with me in an offhand way. 'Oh, I imagine some loss of face was involved. He didn't want to have some kind of trivial confrontation and so made his escape. That's the Japanese way.' If he heard anything, he'd of course let me know. He was sorry that he couldn't talk for longer but he and Masa were listening to a live broadcast of

*Tannhäuser* given by the Vienna State Opera in Tokyo. Wagner was their favourite composer, he added.

The next day I telephoned Katinka and the Shotts. They, like Rex, thought the disappearance in no way remarkable. Hiro had probably found a better job, Katinka said, and hadn't had the courage to face me to tell me. That was the Japanese way. Would I like her to look around for a replacement? Mrs Shott offered to come over to cook me a meal. I politely declined both these offers.

Finally, after some hesitation, I telephoned Dr Kawasaki.

'Your houseboy? No, I'm sorry. I've not seen him around for some time.' I was tempted to tell him that I had seen the two of them together at the Cock Bar only five days before, but decided not to embarrass him by doing so. 'To walk out like that is not at all strange in this country. That's how things happen in Japan. Perhaps, until you find a replacement, our maid might be able to come by for an hour or two to help out.' That suggestion I also declined.

At the Miyako Hotel I drew another blank. The barman to whom I spoke said that he knew no employee of that name. If Kanaseki-san had been one of his customers, then they usually remained anonymous, preferring it that way. The deputy manager to whom he directed me shrugged. 'Sorry. I cannot assist. Such person I never employed.' He glanced over his shoulder. 'Excuse me.' A gaggle of American tourists was standing at the entrance to the bar, noisily arguing about whether to enter or not. Having persuaded them to do so and then placed them on two facing banquettes, with a lot more of noisy arguing as to who should sit by whom, he vanished.

Miss Morita also offered to help out. But when she added, 'I am not domestic person, I am afraid' – something that by now I did not need to be told – I replied that, no, thank you, I could manage perfectly well on my own. I couldn't imagine what could have happened to him, I told her. He had given me no warning. He had seemed perfectly well when I had left for Tokyo. For God's sake, I had even owed him money – having forgotten to pay him before my departure.

She shrugged. 'All this is not unusual in Japan. Such people are like birds. They fly into your garden, they sing a nice little song, they fly away. Maybe some day they return to sing another nice little song. Maybe they never come back.' She leaned forward, hands clasped. 'I think that maybe you are lucky.' She gazed into my eyes and then shook her head. 'He is not good man, I think.'

# (41)

I am alone in Kew Gardens. Laura said that she would come with me and then at the last moment cried off. 'I have so many letters.' As with so many elderly people, her contacts with the outside world are now largely through letters, emails and telephone calls.

'Put on something warm,' she calls out as I am leaving. 'There's a really icy wind.'

'Yes, yes.'

'And don't forget your stick.'

'I don't need it.' I feel proud that, after all those months of using a stick as an antenna to guide me through shops and streets without a collision, I can leave it behind me.

Perhaps because it is a Monday afternoon, the Gardens are emptier than I have ever known them except in mid-winter. The light is oddly vaporous, with shreds of mist drifting from tree to tree or settling on flower beds to rob them of any clear definition. Distant sounds – the clattering of a mower, the squeak of the tyres of one of those electric buses transporting visitors either too lazy or too ancient to walk, the squawks, yells and shrieks of laughter of a group of children in dark-blue school uniform – seem eerily close.

I sit on a bench by the lake. At first I read a few pages of Soseki's *Kokoro* in a new and far better translation than that old one that Dr Kawasaki lent me so many years ago. Then I put it down, to stare out over what – so hard, so still, so immutably grey – might be not water but a vast expanse of metal. A moorhen descends and engraves a dark, erratic line across it. I feel a strange shiver of excitement, as I used once to feel when, up at Oxford, I knew that soon, at any moment now, I'd lean forward to put my lips to those of some girl. Even today I still feel a similar shiver of excitement when I am bidding for a Japanese print and know, as my rival bidder falters, that soon, soon it will be inalienably mine.

All at once it happens, as for months now I have been both

longing for it to happen and half-expecting that it will happen. It happens not inside my head but out there before me. There are wisps of mist hovering over the lake and out of them a vision slowly forms. Firstly I see the huge television screen, and then I see the old man slumped in the wheelchair and the young man standing by him. There are two or three other people present, curators in this strange, beautiful, somehow sinister building. The old man says something to Miss Morita and I realise that among the hoarse, muffled Japanese words, there are two English ones.

'He is asking – do you know snuff movies?'

'Snuff movies? Yes, I've heard of them. Do they really exist?'

She translates. The old man nods vigorously. 'In Japan more than anywhere,' she says. 'But they are difficult to find. Very difficult. For the museum he has found seven.' She turns to check with him. 'No, sorry, sorry, very sorry. Eight. Now you will see snuff movie.'

The young man beside the wheelchair reaches out to pick up a remote control from a nearby table, raises an arm as though in a Nazi salute, and clicks it.

At first the picture, clearly taken with a hand-held camera, sways vertiginously from side to side. I see, in flickering black and white, a room white-tiled from top to bottom. It must be a bathroom. Someone with a white hood over the head is strapped to an upright chair in front of an old-fashioned washbasin with high taps. He – or is it she? – is motionless, inert. Then I make out the narrow, shiny, black shoes – clearly a man's. Six figures, in raincoats uniformly dark and belted and reaching almost to their ankles, are standing with their backs to the camera. One grasps what looks like a metal bar in one hand; the others hold baseball bats. The man with the bar approaches the figure, raises it high up in the air, so that I see its magnified black shadow on the white tiles of the wall beside him, and then brings it down with tremendous violence on the head of the victim. I try to see the assailant more closely. He is extraordinarily tall for a Japanese. The figure reminds me of someone – who, who? Then one of the others moves forward. That dandelion clock of hair so blonde as almost to be white, the sloping shoulders, the wide hips... But surely I know him! He swings the baseball bat. Such is the force that, though the film has no sound, I wait in horror for the crunch of splintering bone.

Suddenly I see it. Above the victim, above the washbasin, on a glass shelf, there it is. POUR UN HOMME. Then in smaller lettering, no capitals, *eau de toilette*. Then below that CARON, and below that again *Paris*.

At that moment the vast television set seems to explode with a blinding flash of light and a noise like a deafening clash of giant cymbals. But the explosion is not out there before me but inside me, in the infinitely complex and mysterious recesses of my brain. It hurls me to the marble floor. It hurls me into oblivion.

*Also by Francis King*

## The Sunlight on the Garden

'Seamlessly crafted with a perfect self-containment and compactness – each as complete as a nut in a shell. A beauty'
– Kate Saunders, *The Times*

'Fairly seethes with incident ... from a master of the short, sharp shock'
– *Independent*

'Sad, ironic, nostalgic and illuminating glimpses into the dark corners of people's lives ... sparing, unsentimental, controlled prose with no words wasted. These are stories of loss, rejection and angst which provoke powerful emotion'
– Carla McKay, *Daily Mail*

'This fine collection will give pleasure to anyone with regard for the carefully crafted and cunningly contrived narrative. Here is a collection of tales which provides many subtle pleasures'
– Peter Burton, *Daily Express*

'A miniature masterpiece, pulsating with feeling, complexity of thought, and the need to make sense of things'
– *Literary Review*

'Every story here is good, every page a pleasure'
– *Scotsman*